Nine Lives by Paul Varjak

short stories by

DAVE DUMANIS

ISBN: 148236915X

ISBN-13: 978-1482369151

DEDICATION

To the readers of 2063, if any.

CONTENTS

ACKNOWLEDGMENT

Thanks to the Walnut Creek office of Marcus & Millichap Real Estate Investment Services for providing me with a safe and comfortable space in which to write this book.

"I suppose they're dirty too, but only incidentally. Mainly they're angry, sensitive, tensely felt, and that dirtiest of all dirty words... promising."

> Fictional writer Paul Varjak, on the stories in his collection *Nine Lives Breakfast at Tiffany's* (the movie), 1960

INTRODUCTION

I've watched *Breakfast at Tiffany's* many times, though I've read Truman Capote's novel just once. In spite of its slick gloss, too-goofy slapstick and sentimental ending, the film version has become a favorite of mine. It probably rings so true for me because I've known a lot of women like Holly Golightly, naive, sophisticated, tragic, driven "*real* phonies" whose biggest fear in the world is to become attached to anything or anyone—except temporarily for practicality's sake, like a cat. As a matter of fact I've dated far more than my share of Hollies, though I've managed to escape the sad fate of being wedded to one. Marriage to such a broken person could only end in disaster.

This project came about because, being a fiction writer myself, I got to thinking about books and movies whose characters were fiction writers or screenwriters. This was at the tail end of a vacation, when one has the time to think about such things. It occurred to me that the *Tiffany's* character Paul Varjak, played by George Peppard in the movie, was supposed to be a writer, although he's presented as not having written anything for several years, apparently because he's been too busy bonking Patricia Neal. But according to the script, he did put one book out, many years before the film is set: a collection of stories called *Nine Lives.*

This book *is* that book.

There's not really a lot of indication about what kind of writer Varjak is, not in the movie, at least. He's tall and good-looking, but I don't know how that would impact his writing, except by giving him lots of opportunities not to do it. He's supposed to have started writing around 1950, so that would make his contemporaries Hemingway and Faulkner, the Beats, pulp writers with literary aspirations like Bradbury and early Vonnegut, and hacks like Erskine Caldwell. I've tried to include a flavor of a little of all of these in this work. And, as mentioned in the *Tiffany's* script, there are nine stories here, no more, no less.

I've also gone with a typical pulp magazine length of 12 to 30 pages per story, since most short story anthologies in those days contained previously published pieces. Of course, this was back when there *was* a market for stories, beyond the stalwart *New Yorker* and the wonderful *McSweeney's* and a few literary journals that pay in copies.

Since I embarked on this project, a friend politely pointed out to me that the novel *Breakfast at Tiffany's*, upon which the movie is based, is written in Varjak's voice. There are differences: in the book, he doesn't name himself and it's implied that he's gay like his creator, rather than a straight man who could fall in love with Holly. Those issues aside, though, he's more or less the same character, making the book you're holding the second one to be ostensibly written by this fictional individual. But that's OK by me. It's not Capote who interests me but Varjak who, over the years, as the movie in which he appears has been vindicated as a minor classic, has taken on a kind of life of his own.

So, here you go: nine stories by Paul Varjak, a man who never existed. They are of the time in which they're set, though there are a couple of sci-fi pieces in here as befits 1959. Prominently featured are the war mentality with its accompanying nuclear threat, dated attitudes about race and gender, and a somewhat mindless attachment to "progress" whatever that might mean on a given day. The result is, I like to think, as bittersweet as it is true to life.

I'd also like to think we've now made it well beyond that dated mindset. But the facts do not bear me out.

Dave Dumanis
San Francisco
January 2013

1 THE FALL OF EL GUACAMOLE

After the smooth, clean, modern jet ride, the taxi ride into Tijuana seemed bumpy and smoky by comparison. Steve didn't mind. He assumed the chaos was part of the ambiance, and besides, he was on vacation now. His vacation that he'd earned, worked hard for. He spent the ride with his arm around Violet, her slim waist compelling his hand as he stared into her doe eyes.

"Are you ready for a little excitement and adventure?" he teased.

"That's what I came here for," his wife replied, just a little too gleefully.

Something he couldn't put his finger on was wrong, off. But he'd convinced himself everything was just fine.

They got to their run-down hotel and, on the advice of the manager, a middle-aged charmer named Ignacio with shiny hair and a suit to match, locked all their valuables and cash in the hotel room safe. "Then you will be free to embark on your vacation without worries or cares," he'd added in his mellifluous, thinly accented English, while his eyes strayed down Violet's delicate but firm décolletage and down her endless, perfect legs. To Steve's surprise, the usually demure Violet had returned Ignacio's attentions with her own icy yet clearly lascivious gaze.

"What was that all about?" Steve asked after they left the reception desk to go secure their valuables.

"I don't know what you're talking about," Violet said coolly.

"You know darn well you do," Steve replied. "We're about to be married." He glared at her.

"I was being polite. If a lady can't be polite to a gentleman who's done a fine job of servicing her, then I don't know what," Violet said, holding up the room keys, safe key, and brochure on "Attractions Not to Miss" that Ignacio had given her in the name of performing his duties.

"I think you mean 'serving," Steve fumed. Even if it was already 1952, he thought, decorum and propriety were the warp and woof of the social fabric, damn it, not relics. He still had a shred of dignity left.

Steve slapped his wife, a good hard slap across the face. He had been taught never to hit a woman, but surely there were exceptions to every rule, and anyway he couldn't have her acting like that toward every Speedy Gonzales they met on vacation. Besides, he had a future as a civil engineer and she knew it. Why ruin a good thing?

Once in the room, they put most of Steve's cash into the safe along with Violet's diamond engagement ring. Steve wasn't happy about the now frozen-faced Violet, slap mark still visible on her left cheek, gallivanting around town without her symbol of betrothal. But they'd be together the whole time, so what difference would it really make?

Steve closed the safe door, and heard a satisfying click. Then, remembering a boyhood experience with a high school locker, he decided to test the apparatus by opening it immediately, to make sure they'd be able to do it later. He inserted the key, turned, and —nothing. The door wouldn't open a hair. Maybe he had the key the wrong way, he thought. He turned it right, left, then right again. He pulled, pushed, tugged. He pulled the key out, examined it, reinserted it. It certainly seemed to be the correct shape, seemed handcrafted for its lock, in fact.

"It's a scam," Steve concluded. "This is how they make their money. That's why the rooms are so cheap. They take guests' valuables and fence them to jewelry stores and banks."

Violet chose her words with perfect care. "Why don't you stay here and guard them," she said, "and I'll walk downstairs and see if I can straighten this out with Ignacio."

"I'm not going to stay cooped up in a hotel room on the first day of my damned vacation," Steve replied. "I'm going out." He fingered the rich fabric of his custom-made guayabera shirt, which had cost him almost a week's salary. He'd had it specifically made for their Mexican vacation – his vacation – and now he was going to walk it around and show it off. He whipped his cigarette pack out of his pocket, lighting one with a matchbook from the lobby.

"With what money?" Violet demanded, nodding toward the safe. But Steve had bought and read a book of 100 Travelers' Survival Tips, and #47—Carry Extra Cash in a Shoe—had already come in handy. He pulled off his left Florsheim and neatly extracted a crisp $20 bill. "This'll get me through today," he said, "while you sort things out."

Violet's face became an impenetrable dark cloud. "Fine with me," she said, with unusual briskness. "You go out drinking and carousing, and I'll stay here and mind the family business. It is your vacation, after all."

"Now you're talking." Steve gave her a peck on her suddenly unyielding cheek and lit out for downtown, crisp $20 bill neatly in hand.

Out on the street, Steve strolled and cracked a smile. Women! he thought. It occurred to him that you didn't even need a follow-up sentence. That just said it all right there.

He looked up at the gorgeous, cloudless sky. It was 90 if it was a degree, a far cry from Ohio's vicious winter. This was a day of promise and opportunity. This was a day when anything could happen.

Then he happened to look down. Rectangular clumps of pink, sugar-coated popcorn were broken to bits beneath his feet. He had been trampling them and now they were nothing but pink crumbs obscuring the dusty, cracked, poorly paved ground.

A prostitute, gaudily dressed in red spangles and fishnets, leaned against a lamppost and smoked. The post had a pole but no lamp mechanism. Probably the city was planning to add one at some later date. The cigarette smelled vaguely of manure and Steve lit one of his own to cover the smell. Rows of piñatas swung listlessly from the ceiling of a market stall, party pink and white and red, while at the stall next door cuts of beef hung just as listlessly, part-covered with flies. Was it just because he was jetlagged that he had trouble telling one from the other?

What kind of a sad person would go to a prostitute on a vacation, Steve wondered? If your relationship with your wife were that shaky, why take her on a vacation in the first place? If, on the other hand, you were alone, what better place to find romance? Nubile young native senoritas just waiting for the chance to step out, crowding the salsa bars; not to mention all the beautiful women who came from all over the United States, no, the world, not just San Diego but Chicago, New York, Paris, London. Exceptionally lovely and seductive women, jet setters who viewed "morals" as a term of convenience, who came here in packs to get away from the rich husbands that ignored them and the society that restrained them.

Even though it was barely noon, it was five o'clock somewhere, Steve thought. He turned the corner and found himself on a street with nothing but cantinas. None seemed to have names and each one seemed filthier, more gaudily painted, noisier, and more depraved than the last. Well, why did I come here if not to have fun?, he thought. This is probably my only time away from Violet for the rest of the week.

He ducked into the last cantina on the block. There was barely room for him between the unshaven men, women in clothing remarkably skimpy even for this heat, the mariachi band, and dogs, cats, and roosters chasing one another around the tables. "Uno cerveza y uno whiskey, un doble," he told the red-eyed bartender in his best broken Spanish.

"No one drinks," the bartender replied in struck Steve as surprisingly competent English, "unless he fights El Guacamole."

Steve couldn't believe what he was hearing. First of all, what legitimate business would refuse paying customers drinks unless they engaged in a fight first? Then there was the name El Guacamole, surely the silliest and least threatening name ever taken by any fighter anywhere. And it was all said with such an incredibly straight face. Steve even laughed, then tried to swallow it lest he make the bartender angry.

"Sure," he said. "I'll fight El Guacamole."

The bartender set a beer on the disgusting, grease-stained bar, with a deep thunk that spilled foam over the sides. "Beer first, for strength," he said. "You'll need it. Whiskey after the fight."

The patrons cleared without any announcement from the bartender, as though they psychically knew what was about to take place. A ring shape began to form as the crowds huddled up in the corners; Plumes of smoke formed above each corner as the patrons lit up cheap stogies, eager to watch the green gringo get trounced.

Steve gingerly entered the center of the ring. It hit him that he was far out of his depth. The last time he'd been in a fight had been in high school, and he'd lost. A cracked tooth, a headache, and an inability to see properly for days had been his rewards. And these people weren't high schoolers. They played for keeps, and got their kicks from seeing naïve tourists get slaughtered because they were too thirsty to exhibit good judgment and common sense.

"Senoras y senores," a booming voice finally said. Steve looked toward the voice and saw the same sleepy bartender who had poured him the beer, only now he looked wide awake and sounded like a professional radio DJ. Any degree of stereotypical

Mexican torpor was completely gone now, replaced by an evil, knowing grin. "El Guacamole!"

Steve couldn't believe his eyes when the bartender then effected a third change. He strode out from behind the bar, gleefully surveying the crowd. Then he proceeded to don a creepy full-face leather wrestling mask, the same kind Steve had seen for sale in front of the sleazier stores on the main drag. Finally, he stripped off his bartender's uniform of white shirt, bow tie, and dark pants, revealing a garish, skimpy green costume and a frame covered with huge, bulging, sinewy muscles like dozens of underground telephone cables braided together. He flexed for the crowd, first the left arm, then the right. Everyone cheered, raised glasses, yelled "El Guacamole!" at the top of his lungs.

The bartender is El Guacamole, Steve thought. And I'm a dead man.

Instinctively, Steve looked around for exits, sweat pouring off his brow and flowing right into his eyes where the salt stung horribly. He blinked several times but it didn't do any good. As for exits, none were to be found: the crowd had him tightly surrounded and he would have had to fight several muscular men just for the privilege of leaving.

Steve looked El Guacamole up and down. It didn't seem to make sense. Where as a bartender the man had been stooped and scrawny, now he was 6 foot 5 if he was an inch, boulder solid without an ounce of fat anywhere on him. And not only was he muscle-bound, he was incredibly evil. Just look at his grin, Steve thought. Only the evil grinned like that. He took an unmarked bottle of what looked like mezcal off the bar and in two seconds drained it of everything but the worm, licking his lips as he savored the mixture of near-pure alcohol and the oil from his sweaty face.

Suddenly Steve found himself surrounded by fists waving 10, 50, 100 peso notes, American five- and 10-dollar bills, IOUs, checks, gold jewelry, a pet rat, and all other manner of tradeables. So this was why they wouldn't serve gringos a drink until they fought El Guacamole. This was how they made their real money. He realized now what an incredible scam they had going. (Whoever "they" were—perhaps it was a solo operation with the bartender playing even more roles: owner, bookie, loan shark, hit man.) He was exactly the sucker they had been counting on, and now it was far too late to get out.

Steve took a quick survey of his skills and talents. He was good at running away, but there was nowhere to go. He'd taken a mail order muscle building course as a kid, with mixed results at best. A generic one-day Martial Arts of the Exotic Far East class had proved similarly fruitless. He'd done some hand-to-hand combat in the army, but supply sergeant life had been relatively uneventful. He did have some college physics under his belt and could ostensibly gain the upper hand by applying the concepts of acceleration, inertia, centrifugal force, but for all intents and purposes they were just numbers now.

He was doomed.

He silently thought of Violet's face and said goodbye to her. In his mind, she wouldn't say goodbye back. That was her all over: cold, grudge-holding, stubborn, and difficult. But she had been faithful. That was what had kept Steve with her all this time—that, and her beauty.

An earsplitting clang woke Steve out of his reverie and brought him back to the here and now. "Here" was the alcohol-stinking, chant-and-smoke-filled impromptu boxing ring that had materialized around him and the heavily muscled bartender. "Now" was the fight that was apparently beginning. Steve had no idea how to box or show off for the crowd; he stood frozen, dumbfounded, as El Guacamole danced and pranced around him in his tiny green outfit.

El Guacamole's teeth glittered as he took a few steps here, a few steps there, punched the air, felt his oats. The crowd snickered, whistled, catcalled. It was clear El Guacamole had been through this routine a few dozen times and was none the worse for wear. On the wrestler's arm, Steve noticed a crude tattoo drawn with one-color blue-black ink, probably in prison with a sharpened paper clip. It depicted an avocado, surrounded by a circle of shining fire as though it were the Virgin Mary. Instead of the avocado's pit the tattoo depicted a staring, all-seeing eye, much like the one atop the pyramid on the U.S. dollar bill. Steve had never seen anything quite like this tattoo and hoped he never would again.

Then came the metal.

Steve hadn't expected it and didn't remember noticing brass knuckles on the bartender's fist, but somehow they'd materialized and managed to collide with Steve's face. He felt his jaw crack, saw a flash of white light like the U.S. nuclear explosion tests he'd been reading about in the Mexican papers, tasted blood flowing like a warm, salty river in his mouth. He went lightheaded and collapsed on the ground.

At that point, Steve fully expected to pass out and wake up in either a Mexican jail cell or the trunk of someone's car—if he were lucky. But then he realized that he hadn't passed out. Somehow, he'd taken a brass knuckle punch with his consciousness intact. He opened one eye a tad, instinctively realizing that he shouldn't let on that he was awake. El Guacamole did a victory dance, making the "champ" sign by clasping his left hand in his right and raising both above his head, first on one side, then on the other. The crowd was shrieking, applauding, cheering. They were all on El Guacamole's side, to a man. The weak, stupid gringo had got what was coming to him. Served him right for having the cojones to step into a strange bar and order a drink.

Peering out from closed lids, Steve knew he had nothing to lose. As El Guacamole's dance got more and more ridiculous and carefree, Steve noticed an unfinished drink someone had laid on the floor during the fight. It was a long shot, but it was his only hope. He waited for an opportune moment; then, still feigning unconsciousness, he very slowly and carefully reached for the glass of mezcal, replete with "worm." He took aim and flung the entire glass at the champ's mask-encased head, accurately and hard. He hadn't thrown such a heavy, cumbersome object so far since high school, and had no idea whether it was going to go where he was aiming it.

He just knew he didn't want to die.

The glass hit El Guacamole on the side of the head, with a much duller sound than Steve had anticipated. The crowd went completely silent and some mouths hung open as it was El Guacamole's turn to hit the floor. Clearly no one had expected this turn of events. Then the surprise turned to hate as cries of "Tramposo!" arose. Steve knew no Spanish, but he knew he was being accused of something. Throwing shot glasses was against the regulations of every sport. But Steve looked directly down at El Guacamole's fat fist, until the rest of the crowd saw what he saw: the brass knuckles wrapped around his hand for all his cheering fans to see, plain evidence that their so-called champ had been stacking the deck.

Though in horrible facial pain, Steve was pleased with himself and even a little proud. Then he remembered the reason he'd come into the bar in the first place. But from whom could he order a drink now? No matter: one simply appeared in his hand. He nodded to the unassuming young man who had given it to him, then slugged it down, worm and all in.

And then he got a funny taste in the back of his throat and an off aroma in the back of his nostrils, an evil and cloying and volatile aroma that didn't put him in mind of liquor at all; and then he really did pass out.

#

The next time he opened his eyes, Steve found himself back in a familiar locale. He couldn't place it right away, and he knew it wasn't the wrestling bar, but it was someplace he'd been. Somehow, he was certain of that much, even though everything was dark and blurry and he had a throbbing headache the size of the Flatiron building. The sounds were familiar, too: the hum of a cheap window air conditioner, the honking and motor cacophony of the traffic on Avenida de la Revolucion. And there was a new sound, too: a steady, rhythmic sighing and moaning, in a high, thin little female voice.

Then Steve understood the familiarity: he was back in his own hotel room. Everything was the same as when he had left it: same paintings of donkeys and lovely flirtatious senoritas and hombres in straw sombreros having a siesta, same party-colored bedspread, same wooden wall trim, same stink of cheap pesticides and cheaper auto fuel. Only one thing was different: his wife was now intimately entwined with the hotel manager—the same hotel manager she'd been tasked with asking for the keys earlier. Her cries were insistent, breathy, and loud, much louder than the countless nights the two of them had spent together.

Steve mustered the energy to roll his eyes upward. He was staring at the silencer end of a pistol. The individual attached to the hand holding it was someone he'd never seen before, and certainly not in Mexico: blond, pale, lithe in build, a gringo if there ever was one. He was barely past puberty but his eyes were already in the grave. His face was cold, emotionless, blank, barely a face at all in fact. Steve would have had more luck getting an emotional reaction out of the safe he'd locked his wallet in, a safe which incidentally was now as wide open as his wife's legs.

He ventured what he fancied was a clever remark. "I thought if I was still alive you boys might be torturing me about now."

"Who says we're not?" the gunman responded.

And indeed, as Steve watched the oblivious hotel manager ride up and down on his frenzied, panting wife, sliding in and out as she wailed deliriously, he realized the gunman was right. No private Chinese water torture, no closed-door beatings nor whippings, no prying off of fingernails would be worse than being forced to watch what was going on in this tourist hotel right here, right now.

Steve had many things he wanted to say. He couldn't articulate any of them. He wasn't used to trying to be articulate with a gun in his face, pointed by a man who clearly had nothing to lose, while his wife exploded in bed with yet another man without so much as acknowledging Steve's presence. So, instead, he just thought about the things he wanted to say. He thought about the day he and his wife met, while both were still in high school, cheering on their mutual friend the quarterback in a varsity football game. He thought about their dates, the movies, the dinners out at well-appointed Italian or Chinese places, the twilight walks in the park, the jazz and folk music concerts they attended, sometimes sneaking an illicit puff of "reefer." He thought about all the times he'd snapped at her, held grudges against her, been petty and mean and cowardly and unkind. He thought about all the times he'd been stingy with his love, because he thought that was how a man ought to be. He'd thought about their times in bed together, how she'd seemed dutiful but not passionate, and how he excused it to himself as her having an off night.

And still the rhythmic moaning continued.

It was, indeed, torture. Steve had gone on an innocent walk to try to salvage what was left of a day gone wrong. He'd expected to come back to a loving wife, an open safe, and restored access to his money—perhaps with a renewed feeling of appreciation for his romantic situation, his vacation, and his job. Instead, the exact opposite had happened: he'd come home to a man who was supposedly at his beck and call, pumping away at his wife as though it were the most normal, natural thing in the world. A man who shouldn't even be touching his wife, much less making love to her. Steve tried to cover his eyes and was appalled to find that his hands were tied behind his back by coil after coil of sturdy sisal rope, making it impossible for him to obscure his own horrible view.

The hotel manager swapped places with Violet now, something that Steve had never even tried with her in bed. Violet was so rapt with ecstasy that she didn't even bother to look over in Steve's direction, much less recognize him. But it was certainly clear that she didn't care whether Steve watched, and that was precisely what was so grueling about it.

"Who put you up to this, Violet?" Steve tried. "Whose benefit is this show for, exactly?" She must have been kidnapped, just as he had, and was doing this under duress—that had to be it.

"It's for me," she said, pointedly and greedily. "All for me."

"Shut up," the gunman barked at Steve.

"But that can't be," Steve yelped.

"Of course it can be," Violet replied matter-of-factly. "Steve, we've been together for four years. What color are my eyes?"

Were they brown? Green? Hazel? Blue with a little brown running through it? Steve thought and thought, but he couldn't remember. He tried picturing the eyes, but found himself swimming, swirling, drowning in a sea of eyes, none of them Violet's.

"Exactly," she continued. "You can't remember, and you'll look silly if you try." She took a break from her bedroom antics and put on a nightgown, sitting gracefully at the head of the bed and lighting a cigarette with practiced poise, a pillow propping up her back . "You don't care. But I do. Because I can't stay with a husband who can't even be bothered to notice a simple detail like the color of my eyes. Or who goes trolling bars on the bad side of town when he should be on an anniversary vacation with his wife."

"I can accept all that," Steve said. He was just saying the easiest thing there was to say. In reality he couldn't and didn't accept any of it, but he didn't have much of a choice. "But do you really have to rub my face in it?"

"Yes, I do," Violet said in a crisp, clipped tone. "We came here to celebrate our marriage. If you didn't think it was worth celebrating, you should have told me so to start with and saved me the trouble."

And, so saying, she went back to her shenanigans. Her moan was loud enough to be heard around the block and probably clear to the Del Mar race track. Jorge was clearly much better-endowed than Steve was and intent on proving he was more talented, too. His energy seemed as boundless as his imagination, and with every change in position he became more passionate, more animal and primitive, almost more brutal, as Violet lapped it all up like a cat being fed a rich, rare cream.

"That does it," Steve said. "I've seen enough." He attempted to leave but found himself, not just held down, but tied down. He looked through crusted-over eyes, still weak and tired from a chemical-induced sleep, and found a series of sailor's knots to rival the Lilliputians' treatment of Gulliver, reinforced with what appeared to be an entire roll of a thick, fibrous, shiny silver adhesive tape he hadn't seen before, as different from masking or cellophane tape as a steel girder was from a piece of clothes hanger wire.

"Duct tape," said his nameless captor. "Imported direct from Hollywood. They use it to hold camera and lighting equipment together in every movie from Ben Hur to Citizen Kane. I doubt you'll be escaping from it anytime soon."

"What is it you want?" Steve asked finally, when he simply couldn't take any more of Jorge and Violet going at it like rutting, wallowing, grunting, squealing pigs.

"I'm not sure who that was directed at," Violet replied, "but I'll take a stab at it." She paused as Jorge switched into a particularly complicated position involving hands, his mouth, his elbows, and a good portion of his posterior. "We don't really 'want' anything. We're past that. This isn't blackmail, and I'm not necessarily running away with Jorge here even though he's a great lay. But there is no more 'us,' and there is no more vacation. I'm not going back to America with you and I may even stay in Mexico for the rest of my life. I like it here. I like the freedom."

"There's only one thing women like you can do to be free here," Steve spat.

"I know that's what you've always thought of me," Violet said. "That's why I'm glad to be rid of you. I knew something like this had to happen sooner or later. I'm just glad it was sooner. It saved me some time."

"Are you planning on letting me out of this room?"

"When I get tired of seeing the look on your stupid face, sure."

"I don't, I don't....I don't..."

"You don't what?" Violet taunted without even looking.

"I don't understand. How could you have managed this? How did the two of you even know each other?"

"Oscar and I?" Violet said, nodding toward the thick-neck giant holding Steve captive. "We're old friends. Aren't we, dear?" Oscar nodded back. "We met at Barney's Beanery in L.A., back when I was a waitress there and he was washing dishes. When I told Jorge you were going on one of your many famous excursions, we had a little chat over a few cervezas and it turned out Oscar was a friend of his, too."

This was all a little much for Steve to take. He'd left for an hour and a half, admittedly not with the purest of intentions, and when he'd returned his wife was at the very least a loose woman if not a member of the world's oldest profession. If he was honest with himself, he had to admit the scene held a kind of perverse attraction for him. Certainly he couldn't take his eyes off Violet. He loved to see her in the throes of ecstasy. While on one level he found the scene provoked his jealous side, it was also incredibly sexual just to watch the look on her face.

But more than any of that, he wanted to get even. With who, or what, he wasn't sure. To start with, the syndicate that had forced him to wrestle, drugged him, kidnapped him, brought him here, tied him down and made him watch as another man did things to his wife that he'd never even thought to do himself. Yes, that was true. But he wanted to get even with his wife, for turning on him behind his back in less than a day. He wanted to get even with the society that caused him to feel pain and grief over losing something that had never been his in the first place. He wanted to get even with himself, for taking his wife for granted and going places he shouldn't have and fighting men he couldn't beat. Most of all he had a splitting headache and wanted to go home to America, to a soda at the corner drugstore and the latest episode of I Love Lucy and the reassuring purr of his DeSoto.

The pounding and thrusting and grinding continued until the participants had had their fill. Then, sated, a sweaty Violet rolled out from under Jorge, panting, chest heaving, skin flushed and blotchy. She meandered to the dresser, where she grabbed a bottle of cerveza and opened it with her teeth, one of the many skills Steve had seen her display today for the first time. She drank it all in a single gulp, finishing off with a world-class belch that wouldn't have been out of place at a football game.

Steve decided a little more self-humiliation couldn't hurt now. An invisible string drew him to Violet's side. "I can't stand to see you with someone else," he said as though reading a script. "I want it to be us from now on, just us. Take me home to Cleveland and I promise I'll never even look at another woman."

"Sorry, Steve," she replied. "That milk went sour long ago. You clearly came to Mexico for a sweet little senorita on the side. Now you're never going to look at another woman? Well, maybe I will. And men too. Maybe I'm going to have the time of my life, the time you never thought I could have. Or should have. " She punctuated her remarks by donning a stunning black lace lingerie set and lighting, with a hotel match, a cigarette dangling from the corner of her lips. "Oh yes, I'm going to have fun, you can be sure of that."

"I don't doubt it," Steve said, "but why can't we have fun together?"

"Because we're beyond that now," Violet declared, a goddess from some lofty cloud universe.

Steve began to put an arm around Violet's shoulder, the way he always did when they were on the verge of making up. But a fist came out of nowhere and nearly fractured his cheekbone, leaving him blind in one eye—temporarily, he hoped.

"Lo siento, senor," said a short man with a black fedora and horrible skin. He smiled, but it was a cruel smile, no stranger to torture. Clearly it was he who had done the punching, he who barely looked like he could summon the power to crush a cockroach.

Steve had barely recovered from the punch when the fedora's partner, a tall, fat, unusually pale Mexican wearing an incongruously small Hawaiian shirt, whipped a pistol out of his pants.

"I'm an American," Steve warned.

"That is your problem," Hawaiian shirt replied in strangely unaccented English. If he were indeed Mexican by birth, he might have been raised in Indiana. Yet there were unnerving pauses between the words and syllables – the speech of a man who had learned a foreign language by class and scored straight A's. A spy, perhaps, though for whose side it was hard to tell. "I have contacts in the Mexican police force, the American FBI, the CIA, the bureau of naturalization, the California state police. Anyone who can be bribed has been, and by me personally. Your disappearance will bother no one on this side of the border or the other. But as I say," he continued nonchalantly, "this is not my primary concern.

"My primary concern is that you have treated your wife like a common servant, a maid not fit to shine your shoes, a slave in bed and out of it. And you think that because of your fancy high-paying job and your handsome gringo face and your pine-paneled 'rumpus room' that you have the right to do this to this amazing woman, this wild, spirited creature of nature that no more belongs in a prison like your house than a lion of the savannahs belongs in a cage.

"And let me tell you something else," he went on, while continuing to point the gun at Steve and occasionally tossing it casually from hand to hand like a rubber ball. "Men are not all the same. For every man like you who has no respect for women, there are ten who do. Men who want women to have a good life, and a good time, and memories. Men who truly love women, not just the agujheros in their bodies. Men whose idea of making love is not simply bouncing up and down on a woman for three minutes." He gazed with rapture upon the now-fully-dressed Violet, who lay on the bed in a lovely summer dress, eyes brimming with haughty disdain.

"Now, it occurs to me that we have several choices," Hawaiian shirt continued, glancing momentarily over at Jorge, who had rolled over and gone to sleep, clearly exhausted from his long and highly varied bout with Violet. "The first is that we let you go. Although that strikes me as undesirable, we may need to do so for our own convenience. It may be too much for you to imagine, but we do have more profitable enterprises on our agenda than babysitting you. Another option is to kill you. We like this better, it's more satisfying, but on the other hand it will leave a mess, which will have to be scrubbed and dry-cleaned. Then there is the problem of disposal. Yes, I would say this is a tricky option as well. Finally, we have the option of allowing you to work for us. Of course, the pay would be minimal: you would get to remain alive, and you would get food of some kind, and if you're very good it might even be somewhat fresh. That's all. That's the end of the pay. As for the nature of the job itself, it would be scut work. Threatening and beating up those who don't pay their bills, breaking noses and legs, perhaps some minor killings. Hit jobs, I believe you Americans call them. Well? Speak up. We're not prepared to spend long negotiating."

"And if I don't choose to accept your offer?" Steve said, as neutrally and nonchalantly as he could possibly manage.

"Letting you go free is not an option, as I stated, so sadly that leaves us with only the remaining choice. Not my favorite, as it can be quite filthy and cleanup is onerous, but it can be arranged."

"I'm a talented individual," said Steve. "I'm not used to doing the work of a street thug."

"That's where you're wrong," Hawaiian shirt said. "You believe you are talented because white men like you rule your country, which happens to be enjoying a period of prosperity. You're like a man who finds a bull's carcass and believes himself to be an excellent hunter when he can barely take down a pigeon."

These words stung Steve, since his cousin had recently taken him hunting and he had indeed shot at a pigeon and missed from just a few feet away. The failure hurt even more since Steve had been indoctrinated from childhood to feel, and still felt, that a man who couldn't handle guns correctly was not a real man.

"Fine," said Steve. "I'll be your thug. Tell me what you want me to do, and I'll do it."

"Spoken like a true coward," said Hawaiian shirt, casually polishing the barrel of his pistol with the bottom corner of said shirt. "But I believe there's one other option that we'd forgotten to tell you about. How careless of me."

"What would that be?"

"You need to be a little more patient, senor," short and pimply implored . "How do you Americans say it? Good things come to those who wait."

"Fair enough," said Steve. "I'm waiting."

"Here's option number four," Hawaiian shirt said, very slowly and carefully. "We leave you alive, and free to go. We simply kill your wife."

Steve looked at Violet to see her reaction. Her face appeared as blasé as ever.

"I'd rather die," she said to Steve, "than be stuck with you for the rest of my life."

"There you have it, my friend. Straight from the source. So you can take the coward's way out and live, or you can take the hero's way out and die, or you can take the slave's way out and become one of us. If I were a betting man, I'd put my money on coward. Marco?"

Marco, AKA pimply and short, nodded.

"And all that talk about respecting women and treating them well?" Steve said. "That was nothing but talk?"

"No, we meant it," said Pedro. "But this is business. Not personal."

Steve stared, frozen, stony-eyed, a weight of a million tons on his shoulders. He could let the weight sit on his shoulders, and die from being crushed; or he could shrug the weight off his shoulders, and die from the effort. He glanced over at Violet, idly filing her nails.

"Here's the thing," Pedro said, "and I derive no pleasure from saying this, let me assure you. We're not in business to teach people lessons, or to act as their just desserts or their 'karma' or whatever phrase is in vogue. We're here for one reason and that is to turn a profit. You're a terrible boxer, a terrible husband, a terrible lover, and you're probably a terrible – what is it you do?"

"Civil engineer," Steve offered.

"You're probably a terrible civil engineer," Pedro pronounced with a laugh, "although they let you keep your job because you're the right age and the right height and the right color and the right religion. So I humbly suggest that you leave your terrible life and join us."

"The Mexican syndicate?"

"Yes, very good, the Mexican syndicate. We're very loyal to those who are loyal to us. Isn't that right, Marco?"

"Si, very loyal."

"Even if they're disloyal traitors who have slept with our wives, not once but numerous times. Isn't that right, Marco?"

Marco looked down. "Si," he said reluctantly.

"So I ask you again: are you in?"

Steve looked around. The room seemed to have shrunk around him.

"Yeah," he said. "I'm in."

"A wise choice," Pedro said, winking at his colleague. "Who knows? You may even get a promotion."

Steve said nothing.

"What's the matter, my friend? Aren't you happy? You saved both your wife's life and your own, and a fulfilling career awaits you."

Again, Steve was silent.

"Such gratitude that he has no words to express it. But never mind that. A car is waiting downstairs for you, a brown Oldsmobile. I suggest you take it. Marco, kindly help our friend take the suggestion."

Marco sliced open the ropes with a switchblade about as long as his arm—first the ones binding Steve's arms to his torso, then the ones around his hands and feet. Then he left, wrapping an arm around Steve's shoulder as though they were the best of friends—old war buddies, maybe. At the same time, using the other hand, he discreetly pointed the muzzle of his own gun at Steve's left kidney.

All this trouble over a woman, Steve thought as he fought through the muck of his despair. Nearly killing a man over her dignity, then making him a slave. It was truly un-American, he thought. But then again, he wasn't in America. He was in Mexico. Mexico, where it apparently meant nothing that you spent virtually your entire salary buying your wife shiny new appliances. Mexico, where a man apparently had no rights at all. Mexico, where a vow meant nothing. All he asked was that he be allowed to be a man once in a while. Was that so very much?

"Bye, Steve," Violet called, giving him a salute that he hadn't seen since his Korean tour of duty had ended. He wanted to call her something that had the word "ungrateful" in it, but under the watchful eye of his hosts, thought the better of it.

Marco took Steve out to the brown Olds, which was idling in broad daylight right outside the lobby. Evidently these fellows, whoever they were, had some kind of deal going with the hotel management. The chauffeur, another enormous gorilla of a man in slicked-back hair and a slick suit, got out and opened the door, and Marco ensured that Steve got into the back seat first, once again prodding him with his pistol.

"Okay," Steve said as he slid over to the left on the polished red leather seats. "I get it."

"I don't think you do," Marco said. "And I don't think you ever will."

"You don't, eh? And who are you?" Steve demanded, his reserve finally breaking. "I read the news. Women are treated terribly in Mexico. They're strangled, beaten, abused, taken advantage of, forced into shady lives. How dare you take the moral high ground with me. Do you understand that my wife just cheated on me?"

"She's been cheating on you mentally for a long time before this," Marco said. "And what you read in the papers is not the whole truth. Yes, we have our share of abuse, murder, prostitution. But ours is an ancient society. To us, women are goddesses. Before she became the Virgin Mary, Guadalupe was a goddess—not just the mother of your pale, skinny, talkative Christian god. And there were others. We revere women, even fear them. They have powers no man could possibly have, powers that come with their ability to create life and must be respected."

"Sure, the power to go crazy once a month," Steve muttered.

"It is too late for jokes," Marco replied ominously.

"What is that supposed to mean?" Steve said. He glanced out the window and they were now doing 80 if they were doing a mile—past unmarked and shady sewage treatment plants, factories, and warehouses. "And where are you taking me? I thought you were giving me the option to, to work for you. Start a new career."

"That is not on the menu."

"But I was told—"

"That is not on the menu."

And they sped up, until they were going 100. Then 110. Then 120. Steve was afraid the engine would literally blow up on them. To make matters worse, the exhaust system was on the fritz and the smell of cheap Mexican gasoline was filling the car. Steve felt dizzy, weak.

He tried to focus on something in the distance, as he had learned to do when he felt motion-sick, and his eyes lit on an 18-wheeler up ahead, going about one-third their own speed.

Marco's words were echoing in Steve's brain like a cheaply produced radio ad played in a tunnel, fading in and out, but all in perfect English:

"You see, Senor, my wife just left me. That's a difficult blow for any man to take. But here is the difference between you and me. I understood that it was my fault, not hers. I cheated on her, not with one woman, but with dozens. And why did I do this? I was trying to prove to myself that I was a man! But now, 20 or 30 adventures later, I feel no more a man than I did before. I broke some hearts, perhaps some hymens, but I feel no more a man than before. How does one really prove his manhood? That's easy. The same way that soldiers and bullfighters and sailors and other honorable men have been doing so for thousands, perhaps millions of years. By being willing to die."

"To die for what they know is right," Steve added, hoping to buy himself a little breathing room.

"No," said Marco proudly. "Just to die."

And the Olds continued to roll faster and faster toward Mexico City, as the back of the 18-wheeler, taking its sweet time, loomed large on the horizon.

2 MARJORIE AND TAD AT THE END OF THE WORLD

Lights were flashing, illuminating Tad's face—first red, then blue, then yellow, then pink. Pink? Really? Who'd thought of that? It was another drill, another in the long series of drills at the Monta Loma Nuclear Power Plant. When the lights flashed and the sirens screamed, as they were doing now, it was time to get out.

As a matter of fact it was time for Tad to get out of a lot of things, he thought as he put on his protective suit and boots and followed the flashing floor lights toward the exit. Time to get out of the cultural desert that was Monta Loma circa 1980 A.D. Time to get out of his boring dead-end job. Time to get out of his five-year relationship with his fiancée Gretel, a relationship that would surely end in disaster if they were actually to get married. Time to get out of the state, out of his mind, and out of his life.

It hadn't always been this way, Tad thought as his stood outside his office window and lit a cigarette right next to the prominent no-smoking sign no one obeyed. He'd got this job straight out of college, which he'd attended courtesy of the G.I. Bill. Compared to the soda jerk, bagboy and waiter jobs he'd had up until then, it had seemed like heaven. Although the pay had actually been lower initially than his tips as a waiter at Le Bistro, the fanciest restaurant in the Monta Loma area, it had gone up quickly as he assumed seniority including lead responsibility in case of emergency. Of course, no one ever expected one to actually occur, since nuclear power was well-known to be proven safe, accident-proof and too cheap to meter.

Tad's secretary Marjorie sidled up to him. She was about half his height with a little extra padding in all the right places—fine for someone who liked that sort of thing, Tad sniffed to himself. She put her hand on the small of his back. How forward can you get, Tad thought. "I always wonder," Marjorie said, "how we would do at surviving an emergency. Just the two of us, trapped in there for days. Maybe weeks." She breathed a little sigh.

"I'd like to think we'd make it," said Tad, trying not to sound too blasé. "The food might get boring, but my training was pretty thorough. At the very least we'd be able to keep each other company," he added, trying to sound gentlemanly but immediately realizing he'd said the wrong thing.

"That reminds me," Marjorie solicited cattily, "how's Gretel these days?"

"She's fine."

"Still planning for the Big Day?"

"Last time I heard." Tad managed a sly smile.

"Five years is a long time."

"Yup," Tad agreed. "Sure is." He played the gentleman and held his slim gold lighter to Marjorie's cigarette.

They were silent while Marjorie took several deep, hungry drags. Then two short whistles blew, indicating that it was time for the drill to end.

"Well," Tad said.

"Well," Marjorie agreed. And they trudged back in.

Hope springs eternal, Tad thought. Marjorie wasn't the first secretary who'd shown interest in him, of course. He was tall and fairly good-looking, and had a pretty good tailor to boot. There had been Cynthia, and before her Mary Sue, and before her Prudence. Each had been quite attractive in her own way, and each had fawned over him in a way that revealed she didn't really care whether he was engaged or to whom or for how long or, especially, why. And each had been heartbroken, though she'd been determined not to show it. This pattern, Tad knew, was partially responsible for the unusually heavy turnover at the secretarial desk.

Tad sat back down and took a good look at his wall calendar. The calendar dates were tiny, simple numbers blocked off in months, but the calendar itself spanned years. Each day was crossed off with a red grease pencil. The idea was to track the plant's safety record. Every day with a red grease mark through it had been a safe, uneventful one. And uneventful, in Tad's book, was good. He often liked to say, with a certain slyness, that if he did his job right no one would notice him. And, except for the revolving door of secretaries entering and leaving the office every few months, no one really did.

It had been almost ten years for Tad, an enviable record. Styles had changed—suits and sport coats had changed cut and fabric, fedoras and porkpies had come and gone with bowlers being the latest rage—but Tad had sat there, twiddling knobs and dials and levers, and every so often feeding IBM punch cards into the computer that took up most of the office he worked in, keeping the plant humming so all of Southern California's housewives could enjoy safe, affordable atomic power for their washer/dryer/ironers and food reconstitution units and home assistance robots. There was even some silly talk of electric cars, though the thought of plugging in his shiny new 1980 Nash Rambler made Tad laugh.

Tad looked up at the reliable Timex wall clock. It was already 4:45, the drill having taken a good chunk out of everyone's day. He looked up, yawned, stretched, and noticed Marjorie at her desk, trying to catch his eye.

"Big day, with the drill and all," she said.

"Sure was."

"Care to buy me a beer after work?"

"Sure, why not?" It wasn't in Tad's nature to be impolite or unsociable. He knew Marjorie harbored false hopes about him. Maybe this was his chance to put them to rest. Yes, that was it. See not a problem, but an opportunity, as that smarmy Dale Carnegie would have put it. Once Marjorie had seen him at his most flamboyant, wielding a perfectly mixed and chilled grasshopper in one hand and a wand of a cigarette in the other, laughing loud and shrill, she'd understand that she was barking up the wrong tree. That the two of them could be good friends and co-workers, but no more, and that he and his fiancée had a very different sort of understanding than the one she believed them to have.

A minute or so after the clock clicked five, the two of them were out the door, with Tad helping Marjorie on with her coat in a most genteel way.

At Rosie's, the local Irish tavern just 15 minutes down the superfreeway, Tad ordered a beer—with several brawny construction workers at the next table, he didn't want to call attention to himself by calling for a sweet drink—and Marjorie followed suit. She downed the entire thing almost immediately and ordered a second. Tad gazed in wonderment, wondering where it all went. Marjorie was small and, though solidly built, she was far from enormous. The answer came out a few minutes later as she became more extroverted, even unpredictable: standing up and pacing, making pronouncements and declarations about everything from the price of peanut butter to the trouble with men, and at one point even managing to sit on the bar – not at the bar, but *on* it, so she could hold forth on what a fraud such-and-such a writer was and why he should certainly never be allowed on 3D television again.

At last, when she was finished with her rant, Marjorie, a smug smile of release on her face as if to say, "There, I said it in front of my boss and I don't care who knows it," cozied up to Tad. While she wasn't sitting in his lap, precisely, she was close enough that she would have made him a little uncomfortable had she been his cup of tea. "So," she said teasingly, "what do *you* think? I'll bet a worldly, educated professional like you has a lot of opinions on the subject." Tad had forgotten what the subject was, but the only opinion he really felt like expressing was that it was time to go home and watch *This Is Your Life*, now in its 40th year.

"You're getting a little tipsy, don't you think?" he asked Marjorie gently.

"Now, now," she scolded him playfully. "You're my boss, not my father. As long as I show up for work tomorrow with a nice bright smile on my face, it should be all the same to you."

"I'm just saying that on a work night, it might be a good idea to stop after four drinks."

"Gee, I had no idea you could be such a wet blanket," Marjorie reprimanded him. "So I've had four drinks. It's not the end of the world." She looked up at him longingly, plaintively, even a little guiltily, as though she were secretly begging him to spank her for some imagined wrong. Yes, a spanking, Tad thought. She'd probably enjoy that very much. *Quel domage*, he would not.

The room suddenly got a little bit darker. The ambient light provided by the bar's outdated 2D television had dimmed slightly. Tad looked up at the TV, expecting it to be showing a dark scene from an old gangster movie. Instead, what he saw unnerved him even more than it probably did most people who were watching that channel, or any other, at the same time. It was a Civil Defense warning, complete with the CD-in-a-triangle symbol. But this wasn't the usual test of the emergency broadcast system. This was real.

The television began to release the ungodly two-tone whine that everyone had grown used to hearing during Civil Defense commercials, mostly on Sunday mornings or right before signoff. Tad and Marjorie both put their hands on the sides of their heads, but the earsplitting drone easily penetrated. The bartender, looking slightly irritated, picked up the sonic remote and tried switching channels, but all of them were broadcasting the same annoying noise and symbol.

"TV bastards," the bartender muttered. "They must all be working from the same schedule."

Tad scanned the room. The bartender was still mildly annoyed, waiting for the "commercial" to be over, and the construction workers continued to talk over the din as though it wasn't even happening, laughing at each other's filthy and derisory jokes. Then there was Marjorie, and himself, and that was it. No one else in the entire bar. All of them could vaporize and no one would care the least little bit.

And now, it seemed, they were about to.

"That's odd," Marjorie said, echoing the bartender's sentiment. "That emergency test commercial has been on for three or four minutes now. Don't they usually stop after one?"

"They do," said Tad, "if they're tests."

Marjorie's entire face suddenly changed. This wasn't something he took pleasure in. He might have, under different circumstances —might have enjoyed witnessing the face of this woman, who assumed so much and used her intellect so little, as it transformed from smug and seductive as a movie star to puzzled, panicked, and hopeless. But that would have been in a different context entirely. A context that said normal life could go on as planned. A context that said Tad could continue to live out his life as he was, *dreaming* of moving and changing and becoming, yes, but still safe in his high-paid job and socially approved engagement. A context that said Marjorie's ham-handed flirtations would continue unabated, and that Tad could continue to politely decline them as he had every past secretary's flirtations.

But that context no longer existed in a world which, itself, would only remain recognizable for the next hour or so.

"Duck and cover, everyone," Tad said with quiet authority, just loud enough to be heard above the TV's creepy harmony.

"Who the hell are you?" said the burliest, beefiest, most threatening-looking construction worker.

"I work for the Nuclear Regulatory Commission," Tad lied, in the hopes that throwing this government agency's name around would keep anyone from asking any more annoying questions. "And I expect our orders to be followed or I'll have the National Guard in here so fast it'll make your head spin."

"Sorry, sir," the construction worker replied. He removed his hat to show the appropriate reverence for the stars and stripes, adding a snappy salute and then ducking under the table along with his comrades.

"That's better," Tad replied, and he himself ducked under the table, motioning Marjorie to follow suit. "And bartender," he added from beneath the heavy oak tabletop, "turn that damned television off. Nuclear Regulatory Commission orders," he bellowed. He whipped his ID badge out of his pocket and flashed it. Fortunately it was too far from the bartender to be recognizable as anything beyond a vaguely authoritative object.

"Sorry," the bartender. And he himself got out from behind the bar, still instinctively clutching his white terrycloth barmop like a baby blanket. Tad expected him to start sucking his thumb any minute.

"All of you," Tad said, adopting the same authoritative tone he had heard operatives from the *actual* Nuclear Regulatory Commission use, "are aware of the Cold War and our race with the Russians. Well, it just so happens that they've called our bluff. In less than one hour most of the continental United States will be wasteland, and so will most of the Soviet Union. If there's anything you've ever wanted to do in your life, I strongly recommend doing it now."

"I already done her," said another, thinner, paler construction worker. He held up his beer bottle and the other two toasted it with a loud *clank*.

"I'll drink to that," said Burly.

Meanwhile, Marjorie had gone from her usual rosy-cheeked healthiness to a pale, ghostly white. "I don't know if... there are so many things..." She was frozen, yet her eyes were welling up with fluid and spilling out onto her knockoff dress, onto cleavage she didn't actually have.

"I'm sorry, Marjorie," Tad said. "You're so young yet. You never had children, I know. But maybe it's a blessing, since they never would have grown up anyway. They never would have gotten to eat cotton candy, or go to the fair or a ball game, or run through the sprinkler on a hot August day."

"You don't understand," Marjorie said. "A women who's never had children... she's never really *lived.*" And the puddles in her eyes became full-blown torrents, as she began shaking as though an earthquake were running right through her bones.

"I think I understand," Tad said. "I mean, as much as a man *can* understand such things." He removed the immaculate linen square he always kept in his suit pocket and gently daubed Marjorie's eyes with it.

Marjorie immediately responded to Tad's touch, melting into him, running her fingers through his hair and pressing her cheek against his. "If we're going to be vaporized in a horrible, blinding explosion," Marjorie said, "let's do it together."

"Look at the lovebirds!" Burly cried, pointing at them, and the other construction workers began making wolf whistles and kissy noises.

"Shut the fuck up!" barked Tad. Which did, indeed, shut them up. They weren't used to hearing such language from fancy gentlemen in fancy suits.

"Marjorie..." Tad began, in a chiding fashion. Then he decided that, in light of the circumstances, it couldn't hurt to soften his tone. "Marjorie," he said a good deal more tenderly, "you know, there's a reason nothing has ever happened between us."

"I know that," she said. And it became apparent from the look in her eyes that she did.

"Bartender! More beer!" cried the construction workers.

"I'm duckin' and coverin', like the man said," the bartender whined. "Get it yourselves." And the construction workers crawled out from underneath the table and scuttled like bugs to the bottle icebox behind the bar, decapping the bottles with their teeth one by one. A couple of tumblers full of bourbon were poured, as well.

"So," Tad continued, "you can't expect anything to happen now, just because... just because..."

"It's the end of the world?" Marjorie finished.

"Something like that."

"Well, I don't," she sniffed. "I don't expect that. I'm not that naïve, despite how I might act and despite what you might think. But I have something to tell you, Tad Preston. You think you're above everything and everybody, because you're more stylish and fashionable and you think of smarter things to say." Tad stared at her, shocked by her bluntness and unwilling—unable—to tell her that her slick, dashing image of him hardly matched his own image of himself. "But you're not above everything. You're not immortal. When you die you'll be dead, same as everybody else."

"That's certainly true," Tad said. "In fact, I'll be more dead, since

I have no children who might possibly survive me. But the truth is, I don't want any more of me walking around. They might feel the need to make smart-alecky remarks that I couldn't easily retort."

"I like how you can be funny even under pressure," Marjorie said. She cozied up to him again, fitting her face right in next to his neck. Tad felt more like a mother duck than anything else, but he let Marjorie do it. All bets were off, now. What harm could he come to? "I can be funny, too," she added, lightly kissing him on his face, then his neck, then proceeding down his chest (opening each button as she went), and finally to the fly of his trousers, fumbling like a teenage girl at a petting party.

"Er," Tad started to say, and then thought the better of it. Again, what difference would it make?

They'd both be dead in 30 minutes. Why not make the most of companionship – *any* companionship?

"Petting" is perhaps not the right word for what Tad and Marjorie did, because that phrase sounds like both parties actually want to do it. It connotes perhaps a frisson, a joi de vivre that was simply not there. What was there was a dread of the coming instant evaporation and a desire for some kind, any kind, of closeness.

Tad kissed Marjorie, which felt a lot like kissing a department store mannequin. Marjorie kissed Tad back. Her kiss was warm, gooey, with zero muscle tone.

"I think I may need something a little stronger," Tad said, motioning at the dregs of his White Russian. He got up, strode behind the bar with all the confidence of a man who knew he would soon be a pile of radioactive ashes, and retrieved a bottle of top-shelf vodka and a tumbler. There were no objections from the bartender, who was cowering under the hinged lift-up countertop at the edge of the bar. Tad dipped the tumbler into the ice bin, filled it up with ice past the lip, and then brought it back to the table along with the vodka bottle. He poured vodka until the glass wouldn't hold anymore and took a pass at a toast, thrusting his glass toward Marjorie. "To the Russians," he proclaimed. "Without them, life would be too long and too sober."

"To the Russians!" Marjorie echoed, toasting with a make-believe glass. Taking his cue, Tad drained the glass about halfway. Then, to his surprise, Marjorie picked up where he left off and emptied that the rest of the way, too.

"I'll be damned," said Tad.

"Don't be fooled by appearances," Marjorie said.

From there on out, all hell broke loose. There was groping,

squeezing, unzipping and unhooking. Marjorie took her top off entirely, tossing it to the floor with uncharacteristic abandon. Tongue kissing was followed by kissing all over and below the beltline—first by Marjorie with a nervous sense of obligation, then with an urgent, voracious lust, and then finally by Tad.

"How do I taste?" Marjorie asked, aiming the question at the crown of Tad's head.

"Like a haddock."

"Ask a silly question."

And they went at it, ultimately forming a horizontal coupling under the table, a kind of flesh seesaw with Marjorie on the bottom. Was it fair? Was it equitable? Was it a sincere and heartfelt emotional bond? No, it was none of these things. It was two completely incompatible people taking solace in one another, because that's all they had.

"Ow!" Tad cried. "You're not supposed to bite it with your *teeth*. And don't drool. This is a hundred-dollar suit."

"Gosh, you're picky."

"Sorry. I suppose you're right. Whether it cost a hundred dollars or ten cents doesn't make much of a difference anymore. Go ahead and do whatever you feel like," he added with great magnanimity.

Eventually, Marjorie indicated, with twinkling goo-goo eyes as well as hands and legs, that she was ready to consummate her relationship with Tad. She had to repeat some of her maneuvers, and this she did with great enthusiasm if not great skill. Eventually, she succeeded quite visibly—Tad was proud of his manhood, especially since everyone from co-workers to his father to strangers on the street impugned it on a daily basis without even seeing it—and they began to rock back and forth. Marjorie was in the throes of ecstasy. Tad was in the throes of, well, tolerance.

Eventually Marjorie contorted her face, squeezed her eyes shut, let loose a series of pleading yowls, and then relaxed and sprawled, her skin bright red here and there. Other women he had had, Tad recalled—for there had been a few, early on—had flushed easily and fully, their entire bodies turning a lovely cerise; but Marjorie patched, as though reluctant to give herself completely over to the moment, embarrassed by it in fact.

"That was amazing," Marjorie finally said.

"Thank you," Tad said. He thought of saying "Likewise" or something similar, but it just didn't feel right.

"Five minutes to showtime!" yelled the bartender helpfully. Whoops and catcalls came from the table held (from beneath) by the construction workers, all of whom were happily sloshed. Tad reached into his suit jacket, now lying on the floor beneath them as a kind of new twist on the medieval chivalrous-coat-over-the-mud-puddle, and fished out a packet of cigarettes advertised on 3DTV as a women's brand. He gave Marjorie one, which she took gleefully.

"Don't fall in love with me," he said despairingly.

"Why the hell not?" she replied. "We'll be dead in three minutes. By the time these cigarettes are extinguished, we will be, too. I find your warning a little patronizing, at best. Mister," she added drunkenly.

"You're right," Tad said. "Fall deeply, gloriously, irredeemably in love with me, then. It's your right. You've earned it, just by being here with me. But know this. I can never fall in love with you."

"I know," Marjorie replied, fingering his hair. "Don't you think I know that? Allow me the dignity. Please. I know it might not mean anything to you. But to me it means the difference between work having been the mechanical sitting at a desk every day, the filing of endless papers, the typing of useless reports, a meaningless job done by a meaningless animal barely worth more than a dog; or the radiance that comes from walking on a cloud every day because you're sitting across from someone you secretly adore, someone whose voice transports you to another dimension, whose looks and gestures send you soaring as high as a double martini, someone who, in your deepest fantasies, you can imagine growing old with—even though you know they're fantasies, and you feel ridiculous for believing in them!"

Tad said nothing, and Marjorie continued to finger his hair. It felt nice, in a neutral sort of way. Knowing they would die in a few moments, Tad ransacked his memories, searching for meaning in a life which, he realized now, had consisted mostly of avoidance. He'd avoided leaving his job and starting a new life in a larger city. He'd avoided leaving old lovers he should have abandoned long ago, letting them leave him instead. He'd avoided having fights and arguments he should have had, letting old wounds fester, leaving grudges to clabber like cottage cheese. He'd avoided speaking with his parents and he'd avoided his siblings' children, because they reminded him too painfully of life a few short years ago when he'd been cruelly teased and beaten up and pelted with hard objects and choked and sat on for acting, speaking, living just a little bit differently.

Day in, day out, Tad had lived a life of avoidance, and now it was too late to change that.

Or was it?

"Marjorie," Tad pronounced loud and clear, "I'm a homosexual."

"Tad, I told you I know that. I've known it since you interviewed me."

"Yes, I'm a homosexual. A queer! A pansy!" The construction workers exchanged "I told you so" nods. "And I don't care who knows it, because—"

"I said I *know*."

"Oh." Tad's face fell about a million miles. He felt even worse because he believed he should have been happy about this revelation, but he wasn't. "What do you mean, you *know*? How could you? I've concealed it from everyone!"

"No you haven't."

"I was trained at Yale drama school! I starred in *Lear*!"

"I knew, and so did everyone in the office."

"Then why did you..." Fumbling for words wasn't like him.

"Why what?"

"Why did you feel the way you did? Why did you carry a torch for me?"

"Why does anyone feel the way they do, Tad? Human nature. And you're nice, and kind, and articulate and funny. And I dated boys like you many times, in high school, because I didn't know any better. Maybe I'm just a slow learner. Oh, plus you're married. That always makes a man extra-attractive, but then I'm sure you know all about that, don't you?"

Tad didn't know what to say. More than anything else he was just unbelievably disappointed, let down beyond comprehension. He had wanted to make a dramatic statement, to go out with a bang, to put his foot down and stomp it around, but his surprise was something everyone knew already anyway, the confessional equivalent of calling the sky blue and water wet.

"Five, four, three, two, one, *happy new year!*" cried the now-crazed bartender as he raised a bottle of tequila to his lips and began to down the entire contents without stopping.

And then something happened. Or, to be more correct, absolutely nothing happened.

Everyone cowered, and ducked. The construction workers huddled in a brotherly kind of embrace with their arms around each others' shoulders. But there was no other shoe to drop. No flash, no boom, no sign of any explosion at all. Nothing to make this hour of the day stand out from any other. Everyone stood stock still, the suspense an electrical tension in their spines. And the bartender continued to drain his bottle of tequila, clearly convinced that it was better to be ready than not.

After another four minutes of this paralysis, it occurred to one of the construction workers to get up and turn the television back on, just to check. This he did, with the bartender making nominal motions to stop him but much too weak to do anything about them.

Instead of the Civil Defense emergency tone and logo, or the "snow" that would have meant transmitters had been knocked out *somewhere* by an A-bomb or H-bomb even though it might not have been down the block, the TV was broadcasting a simple baseball game. Not the news, with a sweaty announcer no longer nervous but jubilant with relief. Not a special report nor any kind of takeover broadcast from Soviet communists intent on deluging the airwaves with propaganda to brainwash the few American citizens left. No, a baseball game—the Brooklyn Dodgers and the Cleveland Indians going at it, pitching curve balls and stealing bases for all they were worth as if they had never even *heard* of the bomb, as though it hadn't been invented yet at all.

Then an announcer flashed on. "We interrupt this program for a special announcement. The Civil Defense warning recently announced on this channel was a fraud. An internal saboteur commandeered the equipment and is now in police custody. We apologize for any disturbance or alarm this may have caused, and now return you to the game in progress."

A few seconds of stunned, silent surprise filled the bar, followed by spontaneous applause and catcalls. The bartender, now full of nearly half a bottle of tequila, lay down behind the bar to sleep it off.

"I hope Terry's going to be OK," said Marjorie, motioning at the bartender. She was blushing furiously, her blotches more noticeable than ever.

"We can send for an ambulance in a couple of minutes," Tad replied, "but they'll just laugh at us. He'll sleep it off." Then a thought hit him. "You know his name? How often do you come here? I thought you were a nice girl."

"I am, but I still like to have fun. I come down here two, three times a week, maybe four at the outset. You should come with me someday."

"I might."

They looked at each other for anywhere between seconds and

hours – first with mutual relief, then puzzlement, then finally a degree of acceptance.

"Makes you see things a little bit differently, doesn't it?" Tad said.

"What are you talking about in particular?" Marjorie said shyly.

"Not that, although that was – just fine. I was thinking more about my being, I don't know, stuck. I've been stuck in the same dull town – no offense – with the same job, the same marriage to someone I'm not in love with. I feel like a record with a scratch and the needle has just been going around in the same groove, without anyone noticing or caring."

"Yeah," Marjorie agreed. "I know what you mean."

"Don't tell anyone about this, will you?"

"Really? But I thought it would help your—your image."

"People think I'm a solid citizen, a husband and father-to-be. I don't want it spread around that I'm taking advantage of women under tables in bars."

"Done," Marjorie said. "Say no more. And I'm sure you'll return the favor? I'm just an old maid secretary, after all."

Tad nodded.

"How long will you stay, Tad?"

"I don't know, really. Another five minutes, maybe 10, I think."

"No, I mean at your job. And here in town."

"Well..." he began to equivocate, but Marjorie stopped him.

"You can't think like that anymore," she said. "It's stupid." She'd never spoken to her boss that way before, but somehow Tad didn't feel angry or transgressed—he felt humbled. "If you hate your life, if you hate your job, if you hate your marriage—leave. Take off. It's a free country. The Russians don't have that ability, but we do. Right now, that is. Take advantage of it. Quit today. I know you've got some money saved up. Look," she added, taking a stern tone with him, "you almost died today, along with everyone else. That you didn't was a reprieve. So take the opportunity.

"Go, be yourself," she concluded. "Life is too short to be somebody else."

She reached up, took Tad's shoulders, embraced him, and gave him a kiss on the cheek.

"I've always known about you," she said, "but I also know you're a brave, noble, dignified person. Don't prove me wrong."

#

Four days later, Tad drove his car down the brand new Interstate Highway (some called them "freeways") that President Dwight D. Eisenhower III had recently signed into law. What a good idea, he thought. If the Republicans keep investing taxpayer money in our infrastructure, shoring up our roads and bridges, and our public schools where children can be taught science and evolution, why, I'll be voting for them for a long time to come.

Tad admired the trees, mountains, valleys, and hills as he passed them. He was driving east, so he couldn't see the setting sun, but he could see the lovely pink glow with which it infused the entire evening. He felt free, open, full of possibility. So his life was half over. So what! The other half awaited and he would make it better, far better, than the first half had been. More full of variety, more full of pleasure, more full of courage and derring-do.

As he drove, Motorola radio tuned to a local country and western station playing twangy songs about drinkin' and fightin' and bein' true, Tad remembered Marjorie's face. She was the one who had made it possible for him to do all of this. To say a tearful but needed goodbye to his fiancée, to write a polite but most permanent letter of resignation to his supervisor, to leave what he had regarded as the glowing safety of the nuclear plant.

A man whose entire purpose was to prevent explosions, he'd blown his whole life up. It felt good.

Tad blew the faraway Marjorie a kiss. She'd enjoyed their intimacy even if he hadn't, and he was proud of that—that he could make a woman feel that good, when women weren't even on his menu. He thought back fondly to their moments in the bar, and wished her well finding the true love she'd done so long without.

3 A DRIVE IN THE COUNTRY

Lily raced to put her face on before call. She had got in late to the club thanks to the #43 bus—never a model of punctuality, but today strictly from nowheresville. She would have to make up for lost time. She finished her cigarette sans hands as she smoothed on eye shadow, mascara, eyeliner, blusher, then stubbed out the end and applied lipstick. The band was starting up, with Morty the drummer kicking in first, a good solid kick to the bass and heavy on the cymbals, *boom-chicka boom-chicka boom-chicka-chicka-chicka,* preparing the audience for the show to end all shows.

Just like the one she'd done last night, and the one she'd do tomorrow.

Freddie the stagehand poked his head in. His hair looked greasier than usual, and if he'd shaved this morning it had been with a broken Coke bottle. "One minute, Lily." He looked her up and down, stopping on the plunging neckline of her emerald green outfit—the one that had needed dry cleaning three weeks ago and never got it. "Looking swell tonight."

"You know where you can stick it," Lily muttered without looking up.

"I know where I'd *like* to stick it," Freddie retorted wittily, and took off, probably for an empty seat in the audience.

Okay, doll, Lily thought to herself. This is your chance. It doesn't need to be like the last few hundred times, or is it few thousand? You can be poised, you can be amazing, you can put all our years of classical ballet training to use—training that your mother scrimped and save and stole from your no-good racetrack-loving sonuvabitch father to put you through. You don't have to fall into their trap and be Lily the Stripper. You can be Lily the graceful dancer, Lily the refined entertainer, Lily the polished performer. You can go out there a Lily and come back a perfect rose.

"...And here she is," Stu the smarmy announcer was saying, "The one and only Lily LaRue!"

What a silly name, Lily thought as she stood up from her dressing-room stool and made her way toward the stage. I used to have a nice name, a name I liked. Ellen Smith. A nice, homey name. Someone you'd like to get to know. Someone you can share a baloney sandwich with and she won't make a fuss. Somebody you can take to a baseball game, and she'll have a good time stuffing her plain-but-friendly face with popcorn and rooting for the home team. Ellen Smith was a pleasant, personable, respectable lady.

Lily LaRue is a whore.

That's what Lily thought when she took the stage in Stockton, California, at the ripe age of 22.

The audience applauded wildly when they caught sight of Lily. Of course they did. She was a gorgeous women in her physical prime, heavily made up for seductive effect and encased in a skintight shiny green number that would soon, they knew, be on the floor. Their cigar smoke poisoned the air, much of it stale, and their deadened, fishy eyes contrasted with their noisy clapping and catcalls.

Lily began her routine, bumping, grinding, playing peek-a-boo, giving the audience a little glimpse of lace here and flesh there, throwing a glove there and a shoe here with great and practiced abandon. It was automatic now after years of the exact same routine to the exact same music (the band couldn't be bothered to learn any new songs), and any idea about bringing fine arts, ballet, and "The Dance" into the equation simply shriveled up and died, quickly and unceremoniously.

15 minutes in, Lily was naked except for the pasties and G-string the law required her to wear, so that she wasn't, by legal standards, indecent. As though decency on *any* level, in *any* meaning of the word, had anything to do with her life. Was it decent that she didn't have a steady man in her life, she thought, and hadn't since her freshman year of high school and he'd

dumped her too? Was it decent that exposing her body to hundreds of yelping, drunk, money-waving strangers every night paid barely enough to cover a modest dinner out every night—the dieter's special on weeknights and a cheeseburger on Saturdays—and a roof over her head? And was it even remotely decent that, after three years at this job, she still didn't have an alternate plan for what to do after—no real career (certainly no ballet company worth its salt would take a 22-year-old battling 15 extra pounds), no real job – she couldn't type or take dictation—and not even the hint of a man to get married to , with a home, children, everything she secretly longed for. Sure, she'd had propositions—five every night, by anonymous, booze-breathed, disgusting pigs with wide-open wallets and half-closed eyes, their ties askew as they publicly fumbled for her private body parts—but no proposals.

Lily finished her act, naked enough for Jesus if not the law, made a little skirtless curtsy, and blew the crowd a kiss—one of her trademarks. Then she ran behind the curtain, instead of confidently striding as she normally did, flew back into the green room, sat on her stool in front of her mirror, and wept. She watched herself cry, observing her one giant eye close-up in the magnifying mirror before grabbing a cotton ball and some cold cream.

It was a nice eye, she thought as a tear formed in it, starting as a filmy glaze and then leaking out in a weak little stream. It was a very nice eye.

Why didn't anyone want it for his own?

#

She often stayed up late, but never past three. But here it was, four-thirty in the morning, and Lily was still awake. She'd been propositioned by the usual parade of ridiculous, handsy drunks and normally shy family men who dared to take liberties because of the time and place; and many nights she'd taken them up on it, for a few laughs and to chase away loneliness, but tonight hadn't been one of those nights. The gray fog of her gloom was too thick and hard to fight, her desperate awareness of her situation at once too bright and too bleak.

In front of Lily was a coffee-stained newspaper open to the classified personal ads. She circled one with a black eyebrow pencil, the only writing implement she'd been able to find. She licked the tip with a tired tongue and circled the ad again. It said:

American of Japanese extraction
Recently released from internment
Prospects uncertain
Polite, pleasant, open-minded
Object: matrimony
BY7-5433

Lily wasn't really sure what drew her to this particular ad. She'd never dated a Japanese gentleman before, nor wanted to – among other things, when she was a girl during the war, she'd seen countless newsreels, films, and cartoons showing Orientals as sneaky, underhanded, cowardly war criminals, plus she'd heard rumors about their small size in the bedroom department. It was the humility of the ad that she liked so much, probably. In a world where brazen men constantly groped her, confident that their money and status could justify and excuse their behavior no matter how crude, a little sweetness stood out like a sugar cube in a bowl of vinegar.

Feeling unusually shy, she picked up the phone—she had one of the new ones that you dialed yourself, still fairly rare—and, as soon as she got to the last digit, stopped and put the receiver back on the hook. She felt terrible, timid to the point of being crippled; but also guilty, as though she were betraying her side. She tried it two more times, each time taking the phone off the hook, dialing, then hanging up before finishing the number. She felt like an idiot. A hormone-driven basket case. A teenaged girl.

Finally, the 7th or 8th time, she dialed the whole number and stayed on the line. She felt her face flush as her stomach turned to liquid.

"Hello?" The voice that answered was flat and unaccented, certainly not the stereotypical "Ah-so" voice she'd been expecting. Actually, she didn't know what she'd been expecting, really. But not this.

"Good afternoon," said Lily. "I mean, good evening." Then, correcting herself further, a plain, simple: "Hello."

"Hello to *you*."

"I'm Lily," said Lily. "I'm calling because—that is, I saw your advertisement in the, the," she stammered.

"The personals section."

"Yes, the personals section. I liked it. It was sincere, and gentlemanly, and different, and, well, I just liked it."

"Thank you." Modestly.

"I don't really come across men like you too often in my line of work."

"Oh." Pause. "What line of work would that be?"

"I'm an entertainer."

"I see."

"What do you do, yourself?"

"By true profession, I am a survivor. That is why I'm here to take your call. But to earn a living, I design and sell floral arrangements. Posies, if you well."

"Oh." She considered this. "You interested in women?"

"Yes. Did I forget to say so in my ad?"

"No, but I thought all florists were... you know." She made a limp-wristed gesture by habit, even though he couldn't see it.

"A myth, I'm afraid. Like so many others I've encountered in my life. Would you like to meet over coffee?"

"Do you drink coffee? I would have thought only tea."

"Another myth. Coffee and a burger at Jack's Burger Stand downtown, noon tomorrow."

"Sure, I know where that is."

"Don't be late." And he hung up, gently.

#

The man's name, he told Lily, was Frederick Mitsuharu. He asked her to call him "Mitts," as everyone did at the florist's shop. Exactly as on the phone, he was extremely well-spoken without a trace of an accent, which made sense since he had been born, and had spent his entire life, in California. He was definitely Japanese-looking, although there was a trace of Mickey Rooney about the eyes, Lily thought.

"*I like New York in June... How about you... I love a Gershwin tune...*" The song floated through Lily's head, unbidden. Though she'd been picked up plenty of times, she had never been on a blind date before. The feeling was strange, like having a meal described to one in great, lurid, gourmand detail before eating a single bite—then sitting down to see whether the actual food matched the menu.

"You're not exactly... what I expected," Lily admitted over her too-white coffee, wishing it were a gin and tonic.

"I did remember to mention I was of Japanese extraction, I hope," said Mitsuharu. "That would have been a frightful omission to make."

"Yes, you did," said Lily. There was a long and awkward pause as they sized each other up. He seems refined, Lily thought. That certainly would be a change. It might be just what I need after years of being hit, slapped, pinched, fondled, raped, and treated like everyone's favorite Christmas present.

The waitress came by. Lily ordered another coffee with extra cream, and Mitsuharu ordered a hamburger. *He's trying to show me how American he is*, Lily thought uncertainly. *That's cute.*

"Tell me about yourself," she said.

#

I was born on an orange grove in 1930. Both my mother and father picked oranges 14 hours a day including Saturdays and Sundays. News of the 5-day work week hadn't really spread to their neck of the woods. The oranges were all destined to be smashed into orange juice just as my parents were destined to be smashed, in a system where race, language, and national origin determined one's fate. It pains me to say that not only was I myself born here in the United States but so were my mother and father, although you wouldn't have known it from the way we were treated.

When the Japanese government bombed Pearl Harbor, my parents and I were immediately rounded up and incarcerated in an internment camp near Stockton. We couldn't understand what we had done wrong. My mother wept, my father bargained with the gods, and certainly as a 12-year-old I was completely lost as to why we were forced to move out of our admittedly tiny bungalow and away from what few friends I had. The food was terrible, and scanty to boot. There was rice, of course, because we would eat it and it was cheap; but it was mushy and overcooked. Protein was invariably gristly beef or off cuts of pork, not the fish we would have much preferred. Sometimes we were merely given canned crackers and Spam—a treat for US GI's forced by the Marshall Plan to stay abroad, but pure masochism for us.

As a 12-year-old who hadn't yet developed any of the usual masculine characteristics of puberty, I piqued the interest of more than a few single Japanese men interned in the camp as well as the guards. My voice hadn't yet changed, and was still squeaky and tinny like a girl's. My chest and arm muscles were undeveloped, as was my jaw, and I had strangely wide hips. In short, I was physically as much woman as man at that point—a fact that wasn't lost on the aggressive, sexually frustrated adult males.

Eventually I "befriended" some of the larger men and guards in exchange for their protection. In retrospect, I'm not sure that I made the best deal. Intercourse with the men was excruciatingly painful at first, then later became less excruciating but still painful, all the more so because it was a bargain I couldn't break. The only alternative would be to get beaten up even more. I had regular arrangements with a minimum of eight people and oftentimes as many as 12, and all I ever got out of any of them was "protection." I have to tell you, however, that my anus and mouth felt far from protected. I'm sorry. Is this information too much for you?

No? I'll continue.

One winter night, in front of one of the makeshift fires the guards let us build—they had to turn a blind eye, since fires were technically against the rules—my father approached me about this. He asked my how my physical health was holding up, was I bleeding, were my teeth injured, so forth. He treated me like a hero, I have to say, rather than taking the expected path of shaming me and telling me I'd lost all face now and in the future and would be best off committing hari-kiri. He ministered to my wounds with a combination of bootleg rice wine and gauze filched from sick bay or the PX, then explained to me that I was carrying on a long tradition. Every few generations, apparently, an androgynous individual appeared who, because of his talents as well as the duties that accrued to him, was variously known as demigod, shaman, witch doctor, creator/destroyer, trickster, whore, or devil. I was all of the above, my father said, and was in fact serving the Japanese people by allowing myself to be violated in this way—not even a true violation, according to my father, but an honor I should be proud of. My mother did nothing but sit and listen solemnly, nodding at the appropriate moments.

I excused myself at this point to pass a bowel movement. Even by the dim and distant firelight, I could see for myself that the result wasn't encouraging: it was an odd shade and texture, and marked by what appeared to be dark red or black streaks. I mentioned this to my father and he simply laughed and said I was getting my "red medal."

"Where is your courage in all of this?" I asked him, secretly hoping that he had a good answer and was in fact plotting our escape.

"Some are fated to be courageous," my father replied, "and

some are not. I was born to bring up the rear guard of life, but you're in the vanguard. I honor and salute you."

"I don't want *to be honored and saluted," I replied. "I just don't want to live in horrible pain every morning and night."*

I instinctually figured out then, and confirmed later on, what an incredible coward my father was. He basically got a free pass for selling his son out to the dozen highest bidders, in addition to which I wouldn't have been surprised if he'd profited from the illicit trade in alcohol, cigarettes (he was never without one and I saw him smoking all the time in spite of the official ban on tobacco among internees), medicines, Hershey bars, and even sexual favors. The "shaman" talk was just the sound of him justifying his cowardice and weakness, not to me but to himself.

Internment lasted for a few years, filled with amusements which, I'm sure you're glad to hear, I won't relate to you. My only editorial comment is that I felt like a helpless and tortured victim, not a hero. As our stay ended, we were all required to sign a promise not to sue the US Federal Government or hold it responsible—including myself, at 18 considered a legally liable adult—and then released back into the "Jap"-hating world of California civilization.

The first thing I did, when we were beyond the eyes and ears of the outdoor guards, was to kick my father, swiftly and powerfully, in the nuts.

"What did you do that for!" he exclaimed in perfect Japanese. (For in spite of the camp's ban on the language, he had managed to retain his mastery of it, speaking with my mother and then himself for an hour each night in the hope of maintaining fluency upon his release.)

"What the hell do you think!" I replied. "You made me into a running joke, a giant hole to be filled again and again by your brutal Visigoth friends and enemies alike. You deserve much, much worse."

And then I really gave it to him.

I threw punch after punch at my father's face, nose, eyes, ears, windpipe, and solar plexus—iron-stiff, lightning-fast moves I had learned as a 8-year-old boy in the Sacramento Japanese Self-Defense Club. I dared not use these moves in the camp because prisoners and guards alike could have ganged up on me, holding me still and pummeling me; but now I was alone with one man who had provoked me. I use the word "man" loosely, for he had no more moral fiber than a sack of potatoes and no more sense of right or justice or honor than a bowl of mushy noodles.

Soon, my father was lying in a pulpy heap at my cheap black cloth camp-issued shoes. His eyes begged me for mercy, but I didn't give him any. With one clean stomp, I broke his neck and ended his life.

I spent the next several weeks hiding out and regretting my hot-headed mistake. I felt sure I would immediately be arrested by the police and recaptured, this time in a real prison rather than an internment camp. I found shelter in churches, YMCAs, and the restaurants and service stations where I did day work and then slept in back rooms at night. But no blue-uniformed officials ever came to call. I was exhausted at the end of every day, and didn't bathe as often as I would have preferred, but that was the end of my troubles. Jail did not seem to be in the offing. I even fed myself reasonably well after I developed a taste for the suddenly ubiquitous chili, available everywhere for a quarter.

That about brings us up to date. One of the day jobs I took was at a florist's shop. I expected it to last maybe two or three days, during which I would sweep and take out the trash and perhaps deliver bouquets, but the owner, a part-Asian gentleman himself, took me under his wing and taught me the basics of flower arranging until I became the professional you see before you today.

#

"So you're a murderer," Lily summed up. "You killed your own father. And now you're asking, I mean, you want to date me? It didn't occur to you that that's, you know, the least little bit creepy?"

"There's a saying in western culture," Mitsuharu replied. "You have heard it before: judge not, lest you be judged. And there's another: let he who is without sin cast the first stone."

"I know. And I have a lot to judge myself, I guess. But, you know, that's kind of horrible."

Mitsuharu's face fell. "Does that mean I can't ask you out?" he said.

Lily thought a moment.

"No," she said. "No, I guess not. At least you were honest about it."

"Damn straight," he replied in his drily unaccented voice, as he took an enormous mouthful of hamburger.

#

And so they went on a date. Or, rather, they went on Mitsuharu's version of a date. Not that it wasn't American, it was just a little more formal than the rough-and-tumble escapades Lily was used to from the cads, stalkers, and wise guys she tended to meet in her business. Mitsuharu met Lily at her door, nicely dressed in an expensive if somewhat stodgy sport coat, recently pressed trousers, and shined shoes; took her to a steakhouse, where she was served a perfectly cooked rare T-bone with a baked potato and creamed spinach, all so good she cleaned her plate; and finally brought her to a night club, where they proceeded to dance, drink, and laugh and chatter with the people at the next table as though they'd known them all their lives, though Lily did most of the talking. Mitsuharu, for his part, proved himself surprisingly adept at popular dances like the tango, the rhumba, and the samba. Even the new Lindy, a challenge for many of the attendees, was no match for him.

"What should we do now?" asked a breathless Lily after having been spun, dipped, and flipped. She was worn out, yet by no means sleepy.

"I was thinking we could go for a drive," Mitsuharu said, reading her mind. No, he wasn't flashy and exciting and unpredictable like other guys she'd been with. Definitely not the unpredictable part. But that was OK. Truth was, she'd had it up to here with unpredictability. Truth was, she felt like she could use a little order in her life. She was getting to the point where excitement, the excitement she'd craved since kindergarten (where she ran with scissors and kissed little Tommy Flanagan on the lips), was beginning to appear overrated. Organized was the way to go – organized, ordered planning.

So they went for a drive.

"Where are we going?" Lily said idly as they rounded an unfamiliar turn. She spotted a swampy pond, some cattail reeds, a pair of kids playing on a rock.

"You leave that to me." Mitsuharu's gaze was fixed straight ahead, never leaving the road. He's interested in safety, Lily thought. She liked that. It made *her* feel safe. Inwardly, she glowed.

The ride was long and filled with curves, turns, and slopes. They drove around mountains Lily had never known were there and through valleys she hadn't had a clue about. A couple of times she came very close to rolling down the window and getting sick, but she didn't dare for fear the contents of her stomach would blow right back in her face.

"Mind if I smoke in here?" Lily said, removing the pack from her purse and tapping one out.

"Sorry, but yes, I do." Mitsuharu continued to look only at the road ahead. She was craving a cigarette and thought him a spoilsport, but rules were rules, she supposed.

"I don't suppose you have a radio in here?," she asked, snapping her fingers idly.

"Unfortunately no."

"You know, I'm not in the habit of getting picked up and whisked off somewhere where I don't even know where I'm going. That's not a date, it's kidnapping."

"Call it what you will," Mitsuharu said chillingly. Suddenly, Lily realized her offhanded remark was more accurate than she'd figured on. She tried the door, quietly, sneakily, but it was locked.

"And to think," she said, not at all sure it was the wise thing to get too blabby, "I thought you were a perfect gentleman."

"I am a gentleman," Mitsuharu replied. "You weren't wrong about that. But no one's perfect.

"Perhaps my idea of a surprise journey doesn't appeal," he added, "and you would have been happier with a more sedate evening out."

"I dunno," Lily said. "I mean, I don't guess so. You seem like a swell guy, mostly. I liked those fancy places you took me to."

"Fanciness is an illusion. The wise man does not strive to impress."

"I don't usually date wise men. Just wise guys." Lily snickered at her own joke.

Mitsuharu didn't respond. "Sense o'humor," Lily said under her breath.

They rambled on, seemingly aimless, for miles. The hills were getting wilder, with tall scraggly leafless trees blocking out most of the light, and what sky was visible looked gray and menacing, as though it were going to rain any second.

"If you try anything," Lily said, "I'm calling the police."

"How?" Mitsuharu asked. And for this, Lily did not have an answer.

Finally, they reached what appeared to be their destination. It was a cliff. That was all. Just a cliff. There wasn't a building or structure of any kind in sight, and certainly no other human beings.

Below the cliff were more cliffs. They didn't appear to be near the ocean, or any body of water for that matter; in fact, they really didn't appear to be near anything.

Mitsuharu stopped the car and parked it.

"I know what you're thinking," he said, turning away from the steering wheel to face Lily. "This guy is not a nice guy. This guy is trying to take advantage of me. This guy is creepy and this guy brought me out here to rape me. Well, none of it's true."

He looked at Lily pointedly, as though to demand a response, and she looked back at him just as pointedly. "All right," he admitted, "maybe the creepy part is true. But none of the rest of it is true."

"What do you want?" Lily asked.

"I've not had the easiest life," said Mitsuharu. "I've always had to play by the rules. I've been shuttled around, ordered, subjugated—first by my tyrant of a father, then by the United States government, then by a series of bosses. Life for me has been survival: clean, tidy, orderly, but no percentage in it, no pleasure, no reward. It's been coloring between the lines for 42 years. Let me ask you something: surely you've heard of the saying 'a reason to get up in the morning.'"

"Sure I have," said Lily, wondering where this was going. She looked around nervously, hoping she would spot a hunter or fisherman or camper she could scream and yell to.

"Well, I suppose I've never had one. A reason to get up, I mean. And it's not because I've never wanted one, or that I'm afraid to look for one. It's just that life hasn't been *fun*. And it's passed by so fast, and required so much constant energy and effort, that I've never really given the matter much thought." A wistful look bloomed around his eyes. "But now, my life is more than half over. It's been orderly and neat and clean and well-detailed, with all the i's dotted and all the t's crossed. But it hasn't been a *life*. Not really. I need to change that, before it's too late."

Lily had absolutely no idea what Mitsuharu was about to do now. She looked around at the setting sun, the enormous mountains all out of proportion, the trees that no doubt harbored turkey vultures and bobcats and even stranger things whose mysterious forms were the stuff of nightmares. Would it be so bad, she thought, if I let this well-behaved but somewhat eccentric Japanese—no, not Japanese, she had to stop thinking that, *American*—gentleman have his way with me here? I've had worse before, much worse and in worse settings, too. And she hung her head and cast her gaze downwards, toward the floor mat, as if to say, go ahead and do what you like, I'll make no trouble, I'm a sport. If it's OK with you, it's OK with me.

She thought of all the men she'd had. They went whirling through her mind like a trip through time in a B movie. There was Simon, sweaty and pimply, who finished in his clothes before he could feel her body through hers. There was Seymour, slick in his sharkskin suit and oily hair, full of promises, boastful of his talents but mostly talented at disappearing (and juggling four or five other girlfriends). There was Bob, a boring stick-in-the-mud, a wet-blanket, everybody's father in the body of a barely pubescent kid. And there was Mort the piano player, big, rough, gruff, long on muscles but short on manners, though he sure did know how to tickle the ivories. After that it was a blur, man after man with nothing much to redeem them; they came and went faster and, weary, she put up less of a fight. Drinking helped and, since she didn't have to wake up until two or three o'clock in the afternoon, there were plenty of opportunities to do it.

And now this sweet soul wanted nothing more than a little feminine warmth in a beautiful, natural setting, to make up for his years of loneliness and regimentation. Wouldn't it be mean to turn him down? She wouldn't be much of a woman if she did, she thought—unkind, unsympathetic, quarrelsome. All he really wanted was to be loved.

Suddenly, and without warning, Mitsuharu reached under the driver's seat and produced an enormous, gleaming knife. The knife even seemed too big to fit under the seat, and Lily wondered how he had managed to hide it there. Her first reaction was to scream, which she did. Clearly she had misjudged this man. He was insane and meant to slaughter her like a cow. Like the cow she was, she thought bitterly, giving milk for free to everyone who asked for it, in whatever flavor they wanted be it pasteurized, chocolate or skim.

"Don't be alarmed," said Mitsuharu. "This isn't for you. It's for me." And so saying, he slid the knife right into his belly.

"Waaaaaaaaaaaaaa," Mitsuharu screamed. And Lily, who had already screamed once, joined him.

The knife penetrated. Blood proceeded to spill out, not in a small pathetic stream as she might have imagined it but in a huge, gushing torrent so powerful that for a moment she thought it would fill the entire car. She imagined the rising level of blood in the car, like a kiddie wading pool being filled up with a hose, the blood gradually rising to roof level and drowning her, her mouth and lungs full of thick red iron-tasting goo.

Mitsuharu, amazingly (and to his credit, Lily thought), was still conscious. His eyes, wide open and sentient as ever, took in the scene. The serenity that enveloped him defied description, but there it was.

"You're probably wondering why I just did that, and whether to take me to a hospital," Mitsuharu said. "I beg you not to do so. It would merely prolong my agony. I have committed the traditional act of honorable suicide, or *seppuku,* common in ancient times among Japanese soldiers. For, you see, I do not consider my life to have been an honorable one. This, for me, is the only way out. "

"Why? Have you hurt somebody? Have you wronged somebody? What have you done that's so serious that this is your only choice?" Lily's eyes were huge as she contemplated the moral implications of Mitsuharu's actions. Meanwhile, the practical side of her mind was racing a mile a minute: could she remember how to drive home? Was it safe to do so at night and, if not, how much safer would it be to camp out here in the mountains, where bears surely roamed and hunted for unsuspecting tidbits?

"Yes, I have wronged someone," Mitsuharu answered. "I've wronged the person to whom I should have been truer, more dedicated, more devoted than any other, the one by whom I should always have done right: myself.

"I've cheated, cheated myself out of the life of opportunity and possibility I could be living. I've lied, lied to myself about how short life really is and how I could afford to put things off. I've stolen, stolen precious hours from myself during the day and in the dead of night and on beautiful sunny weekends and steamy rainy afternoons and chilly winter mornings.

"I've cheated and lied and stolen, which makes me a criminal; and now, as my own judge and jury, I am condemning myself to death and may the gods have mercy on my immortal soul."

And, with that, Mitsuharu left the land of the living. His head slumped down onto the steering wheel, leaning heavily against the horn. Lily gave a little start when she expected it to sound, though it didn't. What was I thinking, anyway, she thought. There's no one for miles around, so any problem with the horn would be a complete nonstarter. Meanwhile, Mitsuharu's guts continued to seep out of the slit in his stomach—along with what appeared to be gallons of blood, now so deep it was hard to see the gas and brake pedals.

I'm so sorry, she said to the corpse. I'm so sorry life was like that. She thought her own life had been rough, and sad, and pointless. I guess it goes to show you that you never have any idea what people are like inside, she thought. Not one damn idea.

She was out in the middle of the country with not a person or a phone booth in sight, not even a house or a farm or a building of any kind. So getting help was out of the question until she'd driven back to town. Of course, they'd probably look at her pretty funny there. Two people drive off in the woods and only one of them comes back. And they'd say she'd had a motive, too: pretty young girl gets taken advantage of by a love-starved Japanese, then shows him what for. It all fit together pretty neatly, and now that the War was over public sentiment was tending to slop over toward the Japanese. Everyone knew by now that they made pretty good cameras and radios, along with every trinket and kiddie toy you came across; and Japanese Americans were everywhere in schools and offices, same as the regular white kind.

First thing Lily did was pry Mitsuharu out of the drivers seat. He weighed surprisingly little, especially with half of him puddled up on the floor. Lily had been prepared not to have been able to move him at all, but that turned out not to be the case. She yanked him down so that his head was sticking out of the driver's side door, then hooked her hands under his arms and yanked on his shoulders until he slid out like a drawer out of a bureau. With Mitsuharu on the ground, Lily weighed her options one last time. She could try to put him into the passenger's seat in a reasonably believable position, drive them all the way back to town even though she didn't know the way at all, even roughly, then try to explain what had happened to a cynical, head-shaking cop. Or, she could bury the man confident that no cop worth his salt would ever spend an hour to locate him, find a ride back to town one way or another, and get on with her life. It barely even seemed like a contest.

Lily yanked Mitsuharu's body out of the car by hooking her hands under his armpits, tugging a little, and then letting gravity do the rest.. He was surprisingly light and slid out neatly onto the lush grass—neatly, that is, except for the fluids and entrails still running from the enormous gash in his abdomen.

Working quickly, Lily dug in her purse and wiped some perfume under her nose so she wouldn't have to smell the stench of Mitsuharu's guts and their contents. Once she could smell only White Shoulders, she pried a hubcap off the car with a couple of bobby pins and used it to start digging a trench. The thick, blue Detroit steel made an excellent shovel, and before long Lily had a five-foot grave—certainly long enough to bury a near-midget like Mitsuharu. She pushed him in, covered him with dirt saving the turf for last, and then stomped on the whole thing with the fancy white high heels she saved for sophisticated dates like the one she was supposedly on.

She looked at her shoes. They were covered with mud, grass stains, and blood rapidly drying to a disgusting rust color. Hooray for dates, Lily thought. Hooray for love. Hooray for men and romance and good, clean fun.

She stomped again and again, harder and harder, until her eyes were full of tears and the entire stretch of oaks and sycamores and woodland hills seemed a blur. Why? The word formed a stupid, mindless, incessant rhythm in her head as she pounded the soil over and over again. Finally, she slowed down, panting and out of breath, dripping sweat that matted her hair and mixed with her foundation to make nasty, oily, salty puddles. She looked down. The grass didn't exactly look dewy and fresh-grown, but foot traffic around here was nonexistent. In just a week or two, wind, bugs, and weed seeds will have done their job, she thought, and no one will never know either of us was here.

She knew she was acting irrationally. I didn't kill Mitsuharu, she thought. He killed himself. Why should I have to suffer? I'm not guilty, he is. She opened the car door, fished her cigarettes from her purse, and lit one, inhaling and exhaling greedily, even violently. It's not like I've done anything bad at all, and yet I feel soiled, like a murderess, she thought. I could have left the body here for the police to find and just called them from the city, but no. I felt compelled to bury it.

She paced, making a regular pattern of high-heel holes in the ground. Of course, she reasoned to herself, now that I've buried the body, it has my fingerprints on it, which means any cop or detective who digs it up will think I murdered him. Never mind that his samurai sword is in there with him, they'll just think I killed him with it. They'll look for my fingerprints on the handle, and they'll find them too. She paced faster, smoking more and more furiously.

Heart racing a mile a minute, sweat pouring down her forehead, Lily found herself oddly excited and aroused. That doesn't make sense, she thought. On the other hand, she was in no rush to get back, with everything that awaited her: tedious stage work, tiresome men, cheap booze, bad sleep, bad dreams. What have I got to lose? She thought. I've done weirder things in my life. And with more abandon than she'd ever felt in any strip club, she lay down and began to pleasure herself, running her hands down her body and even unfastening her lingerie to give herself a little more freedom. She little out little yelps—first, far apart and deep; then, closer and closer together (and higher and higher). Just as she climaxed, the moon appeared, seemingly from nowhere.

It was round, fat, full, and yellow. She wanted to lick it.

When Lily was done, she was a mess and she knew it. The back of her dress was covered in mud and weeds. The whole outfit, which had cost 50 dollars at Magnin's, would have to be thrown into her building's fire chute. Her hair was undoubtedly a disaster and she could only imagine what her lipstick looked like. She stared at her thumb, which itself was covered with scarlet wax from her own biting and sucking.

I can't fall asleep, she thought. I can't fall asleep... that would be stupid.

She forced herself up, her nerves still in emergency mode, her legs so wobbly she could barely stand. She tottered over to the car, yanked the door open, squeezed behind the wheel, and gave the keys a turn. The ignition turned over, though the car still stank of blood and feces and guts and urine. Lily turned on the headlights and put the Nash in reverse. The engine hummed smoothly as she gunned it. Whatever else you could say about this Jap, she thought, he took care of his car, all right all right.

Lily drove straight back to town, arms shaking, fingers trembling. She took deep breaths to steady her nerves, her window open so the cold mountain air would keep her awake. She drove around hairpin turn after hairpin turn, much more treacherous in the dark than they ever could have been in daylight, and wasn't even sure she was taking the same route back that Mitsuharu had taken to their destination, since she hadn't been paying much attention on the way. Eventually, when things got a little more civilized, she began passing hamburger stands and pie-and-mud joints, but passed them all up to get home more quickly.

After two hours of driving, Lily hadn't passed a single road sign and couldn't figure out if she was any closer to the city. She didn't remember what few dining establishments there'd been, and there were no other landmarks. Fields of sleeping cows provided no clues. She felt her eyelids drooping down like weights and realized it was only a matter of time before she fell asleep at the wheel and plunged right over a cliff into the Atlantic. How many dozy highway drivers had done that before, she wondered—the car and driver never found again? She had no family, not even any real friends – just suitors out for an evening's good time and the biting, sniping, two-faced company of fellow dancers. It was almost a relief when a barricade of four police cars stopped her from driving any further. She put on her brakes and, true to the tender loving care Mitsuharu had clearly given it, the car came to a smooth and perfect halt.

"What seems to be the trouble, miss?" said the lead cop. He was big and beefy, and his neck was like tanned cowhide with greasy bits of hair dripping off it.

"No trouble, officer" Lily replied coolly.

"You were going 75."

"There's no speed limit posted."

"You were on a winding country road with a lot of cliffs and curves. The first rule is never to drive faster than safety allows. You did pass your driving exam?"

"Yes, I did!" exclaimed Lily, infuriated.

"Unfortunately, we'll still have to write you up," said the cop. "What's that funny smell?" he added, sniffing the inside of the car.

"Nothing," said Lily, turning white. She could feel her heart beating under her generous breasts. The cop leered down her cleavage.

"Smells like something died in here. Seems a little suspicious to me— more than a little, in fact. I propose that we bring this lady in, fellas. What do you say?" The other cops nodded in agreement.

"But I didn't do anything."

The cop shone a flashlight in the car. "That would be why there's blood all over the seat and floor."

"I had a little accident. I'm better now."

"Really. What *kind* of accident."

"You know, officer. Personal female matters. I'm really quite fine."

"I'm sorry, ma'am, but I just find that a little hard to believe. Now, I advise you to come along to the station."

"Am I under arrest?" Lily knew a little something about the law —her job demanded it—and part of it was knowing your rights. If a cop was arresting you, he had to tell you so.

"No, sugar," the cop replied. "Not yet. But you've been a naughty, naughty girl. These two officers and I are going to have to show you the error of your ways. Get out of the car," he added. It was not a request.

Lily withdrew from the car slowly. She was so exhausted she felt like she would collapse on the ground at any minute. Her arms ached from digging and her neck and shoulders ached just on general principal. "Been drinking?" the cop said.

"No," Lily answered truthfully. In fact, this was the longest she'd been *without* a drink in quite a while.

The cop shined a flashlight over her face. "Wear kind of a lot of makeup, dontcha?" he asked.

"I need it for my profession," she replied defensively.

"Would that be an *old* profession, by any chance?"

"I'm a performer," Lily replied icily.

"I'll bet you are." Lily suddenly found herself surrounded by a circle of cops. Were there three, four, five? She was dizzy, unsure. She was outnumbered, that was all she was certain of.

"Get on your knees," one of them said.

"Why?"

"Just do it, whore," the cop replied, not even emotionally enough to be insulting. He sounded like Lily imagined Sgt. Joe Friday would, blowing off a little steam after a long week, all business. Lily felt cold metal surround her wrists and heard the click of handcuffs locking. "We've had a long day. Now you're gonna perform for us. Understand?"

"I understand."

"Good."

And so Lily, always spirited but never the hero, did exactly what she was told. Her mind had felt deadened before—on the stage, in her manager's office, with the mean sometime-boyfriends who beat her and hit her and slapped her around. Her mind had felt detached from her body, its own wandering entity feeling not even the ground under her feet. But never had she felt so numb, so disconnected as she did right now. Her jaw rotated, her lips pursed and moved, her hands stroked, yet she was in no way present. She was 500 million miles away.

In her mind this is where Lily was: at home with her mother, in Hoboken, New Jersey, peeling potatoes. Her mother, a calm, steadfast presence in an otherwise chaotic life, was right there by her side, peeling her own spuds. Her face was one of eternal love, eternal kindness and generosity, eternal patience. It was a face of grace. It was not a stretch to say that it was Mary's face, as Mary is usually represented in religious paintings. Lily, ten years old, concentrated on peeling perfect potatoes, removing every last bit of brown peel from the white flesh without removing any more flesh than necessary. Washing... and peeling... and washing... and peeling... over and over again. Lily was determined to perfect this task, to become the finest and most expert potato peeler in the world. And her mother's expression shone down on her, radiant and beautiful and full of love.

That was where Lily was, in her mind, while the cadre of police officers were forcing her to please them.

The cops, spent and satisfied, left her to her own devices, laughing when Lily asked them directions home. Lily didn't even have any water in the car to wash her mouth out. She drove home with the taste of the three (or four or five) cops lining her mouth and the scent of Mitsuharu's blood and guts permeating her nostrils. She was lucky, she thought. It was a good thing they hadn't picked her up on a murder charge. It was a good thing they had been in too much of a sexual stupor to care.

Lily lit a cigarette with the car's lighter to get the taste of the cops out of her mouth. Once in the city, she thought reflexively, she would go to the *police*; but she quickly dismissed this notion as unworkable. There would be no going to the police, not now and not ever. They would no doubt look after their own, which meant she would face not only laughter and the lack of a fair trial but a possible murder investigation with trumped-up results. Was this suicide by a respectable and responsible Japanese American citizen who had never so much as jaywalked? Or was it murder by a well-known, promiscuous, alcoholic, job-hopping, cooch-dancing nightclub floozy? The answer was obvious. Better to let sleeping dogs lie, at least for now.

Lily was weary and her vision was blurry. The thought of going home and resuming normal life wasn't especially appealing right now, so it was just as well that she passed a motel. The sign, in virtuous blue and green neon, blinked "SLEEP" as well as "POOL" and "BREAKFAST." Well, all right, she thought. I could use some sleep and some breakfast, too. Maybe not the pool, though.

She checked in – the manager was a strangely fat man with greying hair but also acne on his face like a teenager, undoubtedly a hormone imbalance case since no one would ever be that fat without being seriously ill. Lily imagined a world where half the people were severely overweight like this clerk. It sickened and disgusted her, and she certainly hoped she would never live to see it.

Once in her room with the door locked behind her—the key

was the old-fashioned kind with a trefoil loop on the end, and was required to lock or unlock the door from either side—Lily lay down on the bed and began weeping furiously, uncontrollably. She panted and hyperventilated, expected tears but there were none; in fact her eyes were oddly, uncomfortably dry. She had an inkling that she was in fact all out of tears, as though the limited supply she had been issued at birth had run out.

There was a knock at the door—loud, slow, and sharp. Lily instantly knew that it wasn't the short, fat, sweaty manager. The knock was much too high up for that. It was the knock of a tall man. Someone substantial, well-muscled. Someone used to knocking very audibly on strange doors.

It was the knock of a cop.

Lily walked around to the far edge of the window and peered out from behind the thickly dust-covered venetian blind. It was a cop, all right. She quickly let go of the blind and let it fall back into place.

She was in no mood for this tonight. She had had her limit. She wanted to scream, wanted so, so badly, to scream, but thought better of it. She wanted to run, to hide from humanity, to hide from the earth. She wanted to kick in the face of her father, her boss, the President, of God.

She wanted to kill. Yes, that was it. She *needed* to kill.

The knock came louder now, more insistently. It was a knock that said Lily was guilty. It said Lily would go to prison without a fair trial, without so much as a gavel bang. It said Lily didn't have a hope or a prayer in the world.

Lily turned around and looked at the hotel room. He'll know I'm a lady, she thought. He'll know I'm a lady who's willing to do anything for a cop—anything for a man.

She saw a table radio, the table on which the radio set, a cheap wooden dresser, a magazine stand with some old newspapers, and a large, heavy metal ice bucket with an accompanying ice pick.

She walked over to the ice pick, took it in her hand, gripped it hard, raised it far above her head, and—with all the deliberation in the world—opened the door.

#

Be kind, for everyone you meet is fighting a hard battle. - Plato

4 THE EARTH AND THE MOON AND SOMEPLACE IN BETWEEN

Every day was the same for Pop, and he liked it that way. Pop's had been the only general store in the neighborhood for what seemed like centuries, but was really only a couple of decades. But in Norfolk, Nebraska, time was a tricky thing. It stretched like rubber and snapped back on you, stinging your skin. 1972 had rolled in before Pop could turn around, it seemed.

It was 6 p.m., time to cash out the register. The TV was on and they were just about to show the news. Nothing too exciting: Russia still wanted to bomb our asses back to the stone age and we wanted to bomb theirs, but that was about it. Good old Edward R. Murrow was still cantankerous but friendly, and as good a newsman as you were likely to find.

A couple of people showed up at the door: a stooped-over old man with wire-rimmed glasses and a fishing hat full of hand-tied flies, and one many years his junior, straight and tall with a head full of hair and a healthy muscles. Aside from the effects of age, though, the two looked similar: a family resemblance could be detected. Father and son, most likely. Pop hadn't seen them before, which in itself was unusual since everyone in Norfolk knew pretty much everyone else.

"Closed," Pop said, not without a certain restrained pride. Some busy days, he could stay open all night, but that wasn't his style. Closing time was 6 o'clock, take it or leave it.

"Moon landing," said the young man.

"Say what?"

"Moon landing," Muscles repeated. "They're landing on the moon."

"English," Pop said, only half joking. "I only speak English." He opened the door in spite of himself, so he could hear the younger man better. He certainly couldn't have heard him right the first time.

"C'mon, let us in, y'old geezer," said Fishing Hat, who if anything was older than Pop. "Ya bucket of bones, it's the damn moon landing, let us watch it!"

"Moon landing? *Moon* landing." Pops rolled the phrase around on his tongue. It tasted weird, like exotic metals and test tubes and rocket fuel. "The moon – *what,* now?"

"The astronauts. You've been following the news, aintcha? They're gonna land in the moon in ten minutes. First time ever. Man on the moon. It's a historic event."

"Oh. Well, in that case, come on in. I guess." Muscles and Fishing Hat sat down, and Pops whipped out three glasses and proceeded to fill them full of the house special whiskey, his own white lightning. "On the house," he added just in case it wasn't clear.

"Thank you kindly," said Fishing Hat, and the three drank. "I'd better lock up for the night," Pops added, and he went back to the door, only to encounter three *more* customers he'd never seen before.

"This is most unusual," said Pops, half to himself, half to them.

"We don't mind if you don't," said one, a cheerful, blooming, rosy-cheeked teenager. "It's the moon landing!"

"So I hear," Pops said, and invited them in too. He popped open some Cokes, once again on the house. "Drink up," he said. "Make those astronauts proud to be Americans." And the three teenagers toasted the astronauts with their Cokes and drank up.

Pops certainly didn't want any more people in his little general store than this, so he went to lock the door again, and once again was nearly run over, this time by an army of ten: all different ages, men and women, boys and girls, even a couple of Negroes. Why, you could fill a small church with these folks, he thought. Pops prided himself on his modern thinking and let everyone in.

"Moon landing" was on everyone's lips. The store was now packed wall to wall, with everyone enjoying beverages on the house, talking and laughing and arguing to beat the band, the men affectionately punching each other's shoulders or tapping each other's chests in mock belligerence, the women and girls hugging and kissing and jumping up and down.

"Man on the moon," Pops thought. He was 80 years old, maybe more. There was some debate about how long ago he was born, but it had definitely been before people in places like Norfolk cared much for formalities like birth certificates, since everyone knew where everyone else had been born and how old they were. He grabbed his pipe and went out the back way to take a little stroll. The moon landing on TV was a good eight minutes away, and he surely wouldn't miss it just going outside to stretch his legs.

The sky outside was beautiful—pink with tinges of yellow. The sun had just gone down and its masterly strokes were well in evidence. As night began to fall, fireflies became visible, adding sparkle to what was already an almost intolerably beautiful scene. The early September breezes provided just the right mix of warmth and refreshment. Pops turned around and looked at the business he'd built with a mixture of pride and disbelief. The people of Norfolk were good churchgoing folk one minute, rowdy partygoers hitting him up for free astronaut drinks the next, but somehow he'd kept a business going for nigh unto 50 years.

"Pops!" someone shouted from inside. "It's gonna happen any minute!"

Pops wasn't too worried. Age provides perspective. On the off chance that he really did miss the first man-on-the-moon, he'd still most likely be alive by the time the second man-on-the-moon was broadcast on whatever had replaced television by then, and he'd watch that. He turned around, just to keep an eye on the store from the back and make sure the kids weren't getting into too much trouble, And would you look at that? There was the moon in, well, maybe not broad daylight, but certainly no one had expected it to pop out this early. He'd seen this before, of course—sometimes the moon is visible during the day, even at noon or breakfast time, if it's revolving around the Earth at just the right angle. But it was interesting, and just a little bit jarring to look up at the moon and see it shining down, pregnant white and brilliant, just as the very same moon was about to be broadcast inside the store, near as life, with men walking upon it.

"If that don't beat all," Pops said, feeling the double moon view to be an epiphany of sorts. "If that don't beat all."

#

"Mission control," said Captain Bracknell, Astronaut First Class, over his radio. "Come in, Mission Control. We're about to step down onto the surface of the moon."

"Roger that," said the clean, snappy, military Texas twang at the other end.

"Roger that from here as well," added Captain Vincent. Oddly, his voice sounded more distant to Bracknell than mission control's did, even though Vincent was just a few inches away. Perhaps it was just a misplaced helmet microphone or a loose wire, but the effect was disturbing.

"Vincent. Bracknell. We're counting on you both," said Mission Control. "Have you got the 20-minute speech we gave you to read?"

"Sure have, chief. I'm adding in a little personal note, so it's going to clock in at more like 25 minutes. Is that OK?"

"Sure, I guess so. What's in it?"

"You know, God and country and so forth. Patriotic stuff."

"All right, I'm sure no one's going to be too upset about that. Where's Bellini?"

"Right here, chief." Captain Bellini's voice had the nasal intonations of an engineer who hadn't been separated from his slide rule in 20 years. "Minding the store, as planned. I'll be safe inside the capsule while Tweedledee and Tweedledum are out there walking around on the green cheese."

"What do you see out there?"

"You know, little green men, giant blobs, three-headed dinosaurs, 50-foot women with—"

"Hardy har."

"It's desolate. A wasteland. Just a lot of sand with some craters, exactly what we thought. Not a surprise in sight." Bracknell looked up and down his reflective space uniform, checking his gauges and breathing apparatus tubes. "Well, I guess this is it. T minus 30 seconds. Down we go."

"Down we go."

"You know," Bracknell mused, "what I would've given to have watched a show like this when I was a kid, drinking root beer floats down at the local five and dime. Men walking on the moon! That just would have slayed me."

"What's so funny about it?" Vincent asked.

"I was kind of a lonely kid," Bracknell said. "I thought a lot about stuff like that. Rockets to Mars! Time travel to other dimensions! Flying robots! You know, the stuff kids think about. It's a little different from a man with a baby on the way."

"On the *way*? I thought your wife would have had that little shaver by now."

"The stork brings you presents when he feels like it. The doctor suggested an operation, but I guess we're just old-fashioned. Anyway, we're letting nature take its course, and it could happen any day. Could be today."

"T minus 10 and counting, gentlemen.

"Well, I guess this is it. Let's hope our spacesuits work properly and our lungs don't get sucked out of our mouths."

"For you that would be an improvement," Vincent joshed.

"Save the sibling rivalry," Mission Control remarked. "Eight, seven, six, five, four, three, two..."

The two men climbed down out of the rocket, on a flimsy ladder that looked like it was designed to hold a couple of particularly playful nine-year-olds but certainly no adults. The night was pitch dark, darker than any Earth night, which made the artificial light stand out all the more. They made it down to the surface and Bracknell began the speech he had prepared, including the extra section. It's too bad he wasn't able to give the original hour-long speech he'd planned, he thought, but attention spans were so short these days. 25 minutes was just about all the public could stand.

Bracknell stood up in a crater—the surface hard and unyielding as Earth granite, but brighter and whiter—and began:

"Ladies and gentlemen, I'm the father of many children, the youngest of which is scheduled to be born any moment now. I'm sorry that I'm not present to see that blessed event, but after all, a father must provide for his family. In fact, as a parent, I'd always wondered whether I would live long enough to see one of my children walk on the moon. I had never dared dream that—within years, not decades—I would be doing that very thing myself.

"But time has a funny way of collapsing on us, and here we are. The great nation of America and our Lord and Savior Jesus Christ have arranged things so that I may stand here and talk to you from the surface of a world unlike our own—"

"Did he have to say Jesus Christ?" a voice from Mission Control blasted into Bracknell's earphones.

"Why *shouldn't* he say Jesus Christ?" retorted another.

"A surface of the world unlike our own, a world that has not yet seen the proper worship of the Prince of Peace, the Lord of Hosts."

"Who told him he could say this?"

"I did, sir."

"This man got to the moon by way of science and engineering, and he has the balls to prattle on about God and Jesus? I'm as churchgoin' as the next man, but Jesus didn't get us to the damn moon! You *knew* what he was going to say?"

"Yes, sir."

"You're fired. Everyone who works *for* you is fired."

"Yes sir.

Bracknell heard this whole discussion with crystal clarity. It completely threw him off, and he began to stutter and stammer. "... proper worship of God and country, and... and... and now Captain, ah, Vincent would like to say a few words..."

"Four score and seven years ago..." Vincent said, reciting the only speech he knew by heart. "Sorry, just kidding. Um... it's great to be here..."

Bracknell and Vincent's headsets were suddenly filled with dead air. Bracknell had lost his train of thought and now neither one of them could think of anything to say. The speech Bracknell had taken so much care to memorize was now more or less out the window. The astronauts stared into space, then at each other, then into space again. The twinkling stars seemed to mock them.

Jesus, please make my baby a boy, Bracknell thought emptily, locking his eyes on a particularly bright star.

#

"It's about time to go, Pops," said a kindly, deep-voiced young man, tapping him on the shoulder. Pops turned around and saw that the stranger was better-dressed than the average Norfolkian in a spiffy blue suit. Nothing so peculiar about that today. He barely recognized anyone who'd shown up—people had come from miles around to watch the moon landing on television and cadge a free drink if they could. "You about ready?"

"I guess so. You mean they haven't started that there moon landing?"

"They have, but that's not what I meant. Though it's a good time to join and watch, since the astronauts seem to be having some, ah, technical difficulties. Bob Barnham." He put his hand out and shook Pops', in a firm but friendly fashion like a car salesman who knows you're in the market.

"Pops McGillicuddy," Pops said. "Say, thanks for taking the trouble to warn me. I kinda got lost in thought there. It happens when a fella's 80 years old."

"Not a problem," Barnham replied. "You know, I was gonna show up an hour earlier, but when I found out you were showing the moon landing in your store, I thought, well, I can't not let him see *that.* He's waited so long, it just wouldn't be right."

"Well, I'm downright appreciative," said Pops, laughing and strutting in the door the way the owner of Norfolk's largest and most popular television set would just about have to. "Because after all... ah, what exactly did you mean, not '*let* me see that'? That don't make no sense." His brow furrowed and his voice turned gruff. "You ain't some kind of communist, are ya?"

"No, I'm a red-white-and-blue American right down to my socks."

Pops glanced over at the TV. It was silent, even though the volume was turned all the way up. Something had gone horribly wrong with the broadcast, it seemed. Meanwhile, the crowd was whooping it up. Someone had discovered the beer in Pop's secret back-room icebox and a case or two had now been passed around. Women were giggling and cackling, and children were running rampant all over the room with no signs of abatement.

"So... what is it that you do?" he asked. The two astronauts on TV, blurry and fuzzy and grainy, looked at each other but no sound was coming out. The moon looked exactly like everyone expected it to and had been seeing on the cover of sci-fi magazines for decades, no surprise there.

"I do this and that, work here and there," said Barnham.

"That so." Pops was displeased with this total lack of information.

"Funny to think that at the exact same time there's men walking on the moon, somewhere there's a baby being born," said Barnham.

"Yep. Big events going on all over the place, I imagine," Pops agreed, taking in the party and, finally, nodding in approval. Yes, young people were taking his store over with a big petting and beer party; but he was a big-hearted kind of guy, prided himself on it, and if any time was the time to throw a party, it was the moon landing. "People getting married... having anniversaries...having birthdays..."

"Dying," Barnham chipped in helpfully.

"Sure," Pops said, "I guess that's an event. Only I'm not ready yet." He winked.

"Yes, you are." Barnham pointedly returned the wink.

#

"Push, Mrs. Bracknell," said the doctor. Between his surgical mask, his paper cap, and the stress in his voice, he didn't even sound like himself anymore. But Mrs. Bracknell took it on faith and pushed. The baby felt like it would never come out. It hadn't felt like it was going to come out two weeks ago and it didn't feel like it was going to come out now. It didn't even feel like a baby. It felt like a stubborn bowel movement that would never emerge. A bowel movement made out of rocks.

"I'm pushing as hard as I can," she said.

"That's a good astronaut's wife," said the doctor, nonchalantly lighting a cigarette as he poked and prodded at Mrs. Bracknell's groin with several sharp, metallic, and dangerous looking instruments. "You just lay back and relax and don't do a thing. Let myself and the nurses do all the work," he added, making a sweeping gesture with his smoking hand to indicate the three nurses in the room, who seemed to be there mostly to look pretty and hand him things. "Push!"

"I'm trying!" Mrs. Bracknell wept, shook, clawed the air, rubbed her eyes. "This is horrible. I feel like my entire body is on fire."

"Much better for the baby if we don't give you too many painkillers," the doctor replied. "Better for the baby, better for the baby." It became a singsong, like the new rock 'n' roll that Mrs. Bracknell's older children listened to on the radio. What was best for Mrs. Bracknell didn't seem to enter into it.

"Your husband is on the moon right now," the doctor said, "while you're having a brand new baby, right here on Earth. How wonderful is that?"

"I'd like to be on the moon," said Mrs. Bracknell. "I'd like to be on Mars, or Pluto. I'd like to be anywhere but here."

"Spoken like a true astronaut's wife," the doctor said, shaking his head and smiling.

"Let me out of here!" Mrs. Bracknell screamed.

"I'm afraid I can't," the doctor said. "You've got to have the baby first. Once it's born, I'll be glad to let you out with my blessing."

Mrs. Bracknell grunted and pushed and grunted and pushed, harder than she had ever done in her life. She had been a ballet dancer back in her early years and rhythm was not unfamiliar to her; so she developed a rhythm of contracting and groaning that could surely be heard and felt throughout the hospital. All she knew was that she had something in her that she should *not* have in her, not still anyway, and it needed to be rejected and ejected, popped out like an orange seed between her fingers.

"I can see the head!" said the doctor. "Keep pushing!"

"It's a miracle of nature," said a nurse.

"It's a miracle of *science*," said the doctor.

"It's not a miracle," said Mrs. Bracknell. "I did it all by my goddamned self." She tried to move her head, but didn't have the strength.

"Here we go, Mrs. Bracknell," the doctor said triumphantly, his voice taking all the credit for a successful delivery. "It's a beautiful baby girl." He held the baby aloft so that she could see it. It was dripping with blood and other fluids, its fine, light hair soaked and matted, its skin shining brilliantly with sticky wetness.

It *was* beautiful, Mrs. Bracknell thought.

But what she said was, "A girl? My husband's going to kill me."

Then she passed out.

#

"What happened to Pops?" little Lizzie Tamblyn said. She had been staring at the snow on the TV, waiting for it to come back on, when Pops had collapsed to the floor. Lizzie had lived a block behind the store, and lately had been coming there after school with a lot of the other fourth-graders for soda, candy, and general troublemaking. She'd heard from her second best friend Brenda Gordon that there was a big moon landing party going on here, but she hadn't expected to see the host lying face down on the floor.

"Hey, what happened to Pops?" Lizzie repeated.

"Looks like he had a heart attack," said one stranger.

"Stroke," said another.

"I heard tell he was feeling poorly," said yet a third.

"He was talking to himself," said a fourth, "mumbling something about men walking on the moon and babies being born."

The murmurs turned louder and louder, and became a steady buzz. Someone picked up the phone to call an ambulance, but that required talking to the operator, who kept saying "What? What?" in an effort to hear a voice above the din. Old man Birnbaum kept on shouting the address into the phone, but with his thick accent, he had to keep repeating it over and over again. He hung up five minutes later, but by that time the general consensus was that it might be too late.

Nurse Nancy, the old maid who lived on the edge of town, came and felt Pops' pulse. "I hate to be the bearer of bad news," she said, "but he's gone." And she crossed herself, confirming hushed rumors that she was probably the town's lone Catholic. "God rest his soul."

Suddenly the room went quiet as everyone saw Nurse Violet cross herself, even young kids, who got the message as well as anyone. Some of the women began to cry. Under everything, the gentle, steady drone of the TV snow continued.

"He was a good man," Nurse Nancy said, "and a good storekeeper." And, although Pops had been known for a somewhat heavy thumb on the butcher and dry goods scale, no one mentioned it.

Ralph Granger, who everyone said kept a cool head in a tough situation after his son passed away in the war, turned off the TV set. The static hum stopped abruptly as the picture shrank to a tiny white eye in the middle of the green-black screen, then petered out into nothingness.

"He made a good chocolate soda," Granger said.

#

"It's a girl, Captain Bracknell," word came over the headphones from Mission Control. "Repeat, your wife has given birth to a baby girl. Golf, India, Romeo, Lima. That is all."

There was silence for a good half a minute. Bracknell was too stunned to speak. First he had fouled up what he had planned as the first ever impromptu Christian speech from the moon, and now this. He had wanted a boy—there was no lying to himself about that.

The two biggest events of his life, and he had had zero control over them.

As Bracknell looked up at the stars and the blackness of space, he felt, suddenly, small. His *ideas* felt small. He had no idea what God was or who Jesus really was. He had no idea what a country was, even, really. He barely had any idea who he himself was anymore.

"Captain Bracknell, sir," said Vincent, "you're back on the air. America is awaiting your response. The *world* is awaiting your response."

"I thought they cut me off," Bracknell said.

"They did, sir, but no one has ever been given news of a birth in space. They want your reaction."

"I'm humbled," Bracknell said. "And pleased." He chose his words very carefully, knowing he would probably be allowed very few of them. "To be on the moon and hear of your new baby girl being born millions of miles away is staggering. I should not be able to do this," he said, "any more than a bumblebee should be able to fly. "

"Is that all, sir?"

"End of transmission," Bracknell said. "Over and out."

Their somewhat stressful broadcast over, Bracknell and Vincent returned to the ship to debrief, decompress, and enjoy some freeze-dried meatloaf for lunch along with a pressure-sealed packet of what would have to pass for champagne.

"You go in first," Bracknell told Vincent. "I just want to stay out here and take in the scenery for a little while. When a man receives the news— well, you understand."

"Yes, sir," Vincent replied. "I have three children: two, five, and seven."

"That's quite a handful," Bracknell replied. "Must change your perspective quite a lot."

"Yes sir," Vincent said. "It doesn't change everyone's perspective, but goddamn if it didn't change mine." He looked around at the black vastness, which suddenly appeared to him to be more enormous and emptier than ever. "Goddamn if it didn't change mine."

"All right, take your time, sir," Vincent said. "I'll be inside." And he stepped over to the ship in the pleasantly bouncy way that reduced gravity allowed. He grabbed a handle on the side to steady himself, pushed a button to open the airlock, and then, as Bracknell watched, closed it behind him.

"Airlock," Bracknell said to himself. "That really is too much. *Airlock."* He massaged the word on his tongue—a word that certainly would have been meaningless as recently as ten years ago. Then he stood there, watching as Vincent disappeared into the ship, and enjoyed the feeling of being insignificant—of being just a speck of dust in the wake of the Big Bang that, scientists had reported, had happened so very long ago.

Bracknell felt so insignificant, he could hardly bear to be alive. What was the purpose? What was the point? He had worked hard his whole life to be successful and dashing and heroic and famous and, when the endorsement offers starting rolling in, wealthy... for what?

For what?

In the vacuum of blackness punctuated by stars, Captain Charles V. Bracknell took his helmet off. Just for a fraction of a moment, he felt the vastness of space brush his cheek.

It felt like a kiss.

5 HOW BACON KILLED MY DAD

The golden, just-roasted bird sat on the kitchen table, piping hot and surrounded by lustrous potatoes coated in the chicken's own grease, along with carrots, turnips, and rutabagas. Little black dots of carbonized paprika stood out on the chicken's skin. I sat down at my place and drooled at the bird, inhaling its full, rich aroma. When you're absolutely famished, nothing's quite as entrancing as a freshly roasted chicken. Since I was alone, I reached out to tear off a wing. A hand came out of nowhere just as I was about to chomp on it, damn near slapping my own right off my wrist.

"Hey! What was that about?" I picked my hand off the table and sucked on my thumb, which had received the lion's share of the blow.

"Let me explain it to you in a little poem I wrote. You take your food before we say grace, I slap your damn hand away from your face."

That was my dad. I loved him, but I think being without my mom for so long affected his temper. He let little things get to him, like the time when we went out for dinner at Howard Johnson's and he spilled a milkshake all over the table. The waitress good-naturedly called him a slob, and you could tell she was joking since her smile nearly reached the pencil behind her ear, but he took her seriously and got all offended and pouty, down to the point of not leaving her any tip. Plus he made a remark about Negroes like her not knowing their place, something he usually saves for when we're in private and not within hearing distance.

"I think she might have heard you," I said, looking down at my clams and fries, which suddenly seemed too heavy to eat. Dad just glared at me and I knew enough not to get any more on his bad side than I already was.

"I don't care if she heard me," Dad said. "This is Mississippi, not New York goddamn city."

I'd made a face. "Don't be so old-fashioned, dad. There's talk white and Negro kids might even go to school together one day."

Dad's thick, raggedy eyebrows scowled at me. "Be careful what you wish for." He took a big bite of greasy clams. Some of them had been left too long in the fryer and turned a crunchy, bitter chocolate instead of a good, tender gold. "You might actually end up having to go to school with them, and then the quality of your ed-i-cation will go down, down, down." At least he didn't spell out "D,O,U,N." I loved my father, but he was an ignorant son of a bitch and no denying it. Time was when I wished I'd been born to someone else, but eventually I got to understand everyone has good points and bad points. You make the best of what you get. At least I got a dad. There were quite a few kids whose fathers had run off and never been seen again, or had died in the war, or from flu or polio or this or that.

I stared at my clams some more and remembered all my good times with my dad: catching catfish with him down at the creek, batting Little League with him cheering me, watching him build a swing set and helping because I couldn't wait to use it. Good times. Then I remembered crying at Mom's funeral, and Dad trying hard to push back the tears but not really succeeding. Water had *drained* out of his eyes the way cabbage drains when you salt it for sauerkraut, slow enough so you don't really notice but then you come back and there's a giant puddle of salty water under there. I looked at the empty chair next to me, and wished mom could be there to give me a hug.

Dad sat down and had me say grace, always my job except maybe if company came over, and then we dug in.

"How was school today, son?" he asked.

"We learned about long division," I started in, "and we learned some geography, Europe and Asia, and we're gonna raise guinea pigs."

"Europe and Asia are fine, but you'd do better to learn all about Mississippi first. You might be living the rest of your life here. What are the names of your guinea pigs?"

"Lloyd and Jenny Sue."

"Lloyd and Jenny Sue? Where in the Sam Hill do two guinea pigs get funny names like that?"

"We took a vote."

"Oh, I see. That's very democratic." He took a bite of his drumstick. He always took the drumstick when the chicken was freshly roasted or fried. The white meat he saved for some other use—casseroles and whatnot.

I should explain about now that Dad took great pride in cooking our meals, even if they weren't ready exactly on time or sometimes got burnt. He could probably have afforded a Negro or Chinese cook, but the fact is he enjoyed it. There was something about the transformation of raw, slimy meat and hard, unyielding vegetables into a delicious dinner that was still astonishing to him, a kind of magic show where he was both the magician and the audience.

"Hey Dad," I said as he pushed his plate aside and lit his pipe, "can Rocky Jordan come over tomorrow?" I'd often told dad about Rocky Jordan and our adventures together at school, generally over dinner since that was the place to tell stories from the day's adventures. And there were many adventures that Rocky and I had had together. There was the time we were flying a balsa wood glider plane and flew it right through Mrs. Simmons' open window, almost giving her a heart attack. There was the time we turned over a giant log in the woods because we were sure there was an anaconda under there, even though it turned out to be nothing but some pill bugs and beetles. And there was the time we sneaked into Rae-Rae's Bakery and ate up all the raisin bran muffins before she could sell any. We both got grounded for a week.

"Sure," my dad said. "I've never met the little rascal, and he sounds like a good kid. In fact, why don't you have him bring his parents. We'll make it a family-to-family dinner, a real get-together."

Now, you've probably figured out where this is going. Rocky was a Negro, and obviously so were his parents. I'd conveniently forgotten to bring up this fact, because it wasn't really relevant to the stories I'd told—none of them involving sitting at a lunch counter or riding a bus or talking to a policeman. I also took a certain amount of ornery pride in not making race an issue in *any* story, with the result that Rocky's pigmentation had just never come up in conversation. And I wasn't about to bring it up now that my dad had just approved him as a dinner guest.

He'd have to find out for himself.

"Thanks, Dad," I said, and bussed the plates full of chicken grease and leftover green beans. I washed the dishes with too much Ivory while I planned all the things Rocky and I would do the night he came over, maybe even *slept* over. We didn't have our own TV but we would listen to the Lone Ranger on the radio, and Jack Benny and the Shadow. (I wondered how Rocky felt about Amos and Andy. Would he think they were making fun of him, or would he be glad to hear what sounded like his people on the radio? Or *both*?) We would help each other with our homework. We would build skyscrapers with my erector set and build a model airplane. And we would tell each other scary stories and shaggy dog jokes, dirty ones if possible, late into the night.

I couldn't wait.

#

Rocky and I had been best friends ever since kindergarten. We couldn't go to the *same* kindergarten of course, since he was a Negro and went to the Negro school on the other side of the tracks; but for some reason he didn't actually live on the other side of the tracks, but about five doors down from our house. The white folks on the block weren't happy about it, but our street was nothing to brag about. We were just a block or two from the tracks ourselves, with poor folks in most of the houses, paint peeling, eaves falling off, half-finished new stories staying half-finished, rain gutters and screen doors askew, cars up on blocks everywhere. Since the Jordans owned their house, there wasn't a lot the white folks could do about it. Nor did most of them care, I have to say. They were too busy trying to scrape up a living.

I often saw Rocky on the way home from school. I walked to and from class starting in first grade, and there Rocky would be, catching frogs or beetles or starting a little campfire in an out-of-the way patch of grass or making an impromptu fort in a tree or doing any one of a dozen things he just happened to think of on the spur of the moment. He didn't seem to get his ideas from anywhere except his own brain and he didn't care whether anyone saw him or not.

One day coming home from the fourth grade, I caught Rocky trying to hotwire Mr. Babbs' Nash Rambler. I could just see his feet, not his head or his hands, but I recognized him anyway. I'm not sure how. Maybe because he'd worn those clothes before or the sure, guarded way he moved his body as he felt around for the wires. I just knew it was him.

"Whatcha doin'?" I asked, even though I knew.

"Hotwirin'," he said nonchalantly, as if it weren't a crime but just a pleasant activity for a sunny day, like running under a sprinkler or something.

"You gonna steal it?" I didn't mean anything accusatory by this. I was just making natural conversation.

Rocky pulled his head and upper body out from under the car. "'*Course* I'm not gonna steal it," he said. "I might drive it around the block one or two times, though," he admitted, adding genially, "Don't tell nobody or I'll kick your ass."

"I got nobody to tell," I said. It was the truth too. I had no truck with the other kids in the school nor they with me. They thought I was weird, always with my nose in a book and answering too many questions in class. They picked on me and then I beat up one or two of them and that stopped the picking, but still no one wanted to be my friend. "Can you even reach the wheel?" I asked.

"I can with these," Rocky said, nodding at three phone books.

He slipped back under the Rambler's chassis and proceeded with his work. He was thorough, I had to give him that. I'd never heard of a kid hotwiring a car before, and it occurred to me that maybe the right thing to do was to call the police, and that I might even get in trouble if I didn't. But at the same time, I was fascinated to see how it all turned out. Anyway, I'd seen Rocky and pretty much played with him a thousand times and had built up a certain amount of loyalty to him. He was an outcast. I was too—because I lived on the poor side of town, because I didn't have a mom, because I was too much of a brain.

"Well, that should do it." Rocky slipped out from underneath the Rambler. He picked up his phone books with grease-covered hands, threw open the driver's side door, and climbed in. To say he was a little short for the wheel, even with three phone books under his butt, was an understatement; but he grabbed the wires he'd stripped and touched them together. I winced, having stuck my finger in an electric socket once. I could still remember the metallic fire running through my hand and body.

The engine roared to life. "Hop in," Rocky said in his squeaky, not-yet-changed voice.

I thought about it. There was no way he could be a competent driver at his age, and he was driving a stolen car to boot which meant the cops could come after us and put us both in jail. On the other hand, it had been a boring week and I really had nothing to lose.

"Sure," I said.

I hopped in and we took off. Without smiling or in any way revealing that he was having a good time or thinking about wires and engines and such things, Rocky pushed his foot as far down on the pedal as it could go. The Rambler, scratched and dented on the outside, was still a beast to reckon with and quickly passed 40, 50, and 60 miles an hour. Pretty soon we were going 80 down a residential street and I think deep down we both knew that wasn't good news. We were just kind of begging to be caught.

"How did you learn to drive?" I asked, just making conversation. I could barely even hear myself, with the window open and the wind attacking my right ear like a brain-damaged boxer.

"Taught myself," Rocky said.

"Naturally."

We hadn't gone two blocks when we heard the siren of a police car tailing us. "They don't waste any time," I said.

"Nope, they don't," Rocky agreed, stoic as ever. He rounded a corner, then another. I thought we were going to roll over both times, but we didn't. This was beyond maniacal, this was a death sentence.

"Hang on," Rocky said. He floored the gas and we went from 80 to 95.

"We're headed for the Wall," I said in the slowest, clearest, most unmistakable voice I could manage. The Wall was part of the armory on the outside of town. It had been abandoned ages ago and rumor was that it was now used as either a warehouse or a hideout for crooks, depending on who you believed. It was made of solid stone and everyone knew crashing a car into it meant goodbye.

"I know that," Rocky said. His voice was worldly, beyond his years. He'd seen it all and now I was in a position where I had to trust him. Well, there were certainly adults in the world I trusted less.

I closed my eyes and braced myself.

What happened turned out to be the best thing possible. Rocky hit the brakes with great force and, although there was a tooth-grinding squeal, the car stopped short of the wall. The cops had ditched us, probably because they thought they were going to have to deal with a deadly accident instead of just grade school kids on a joyride, and neither one of us was hurt at all.

"Thank Jesus the brakes were good," I said, sweat pouring off my hair and making nice little wet patterns in my t-shirt.

"Jesus, my ass," Rocky said. "I checked the brakes before we took off."

I grinned, but Rocky just nodded once. Then he backed up the car and calmly drove it back to the sidewalk in front of Mr. Babbs's house.

Mr. Babbs never did find out. He probably drank and slept through the whole thing.

#

I hit Rae-Rae's Bakery with Rocky the next day after school. We'd never had a sleepover and I don't think his dad had ever let him do it anywhere. From all accounts he was kind of a strict, sad guy who thought fun was too dangerous to have. He kept to himself a lot, and so did his wife except for going to church. Neither one of them really thought Rocky should be hanging out at Rae-Rae's and helping himself to cookies, but he had a small paper route and earned cookie money with it so his parents couldn't really say boo about it.

We sat eating snickerdoodles, which Rae-Rae did pretty good, and drinking milk out of little tiny bottles with paper caps. Rae-Rae, who didn't have any kids, watched us with what seemed like a weird mixture of suspicion and admiration. Rumor was she'd tried to have a baby with Kenny, who she used to be married to; then he went off to Korea and died in the war, which was probably just as well. There was also a rumor that Rae-Rae was a secret millionaire, that she'd inherited a bunch of money from her wealthy tobacco farmer parents and just sold cookies because she liked kids; but she gave me her evil face so often, with her narrow squinty eyes and her sour mouth, that I wasn't too sure that was true.

"My dad hates Negros," I said as an opening gambit, figuring it was best to just lay it all out there.

"He does?" Rocky said after making sure to chew and swallow his bite of snickerdoodle so he wouldn't be rude for talking with his mouth full. "Well, cheese and crackers! Why'dja invite us over, then? He got a gun, too?"

"Naw, he ain't got a gun, leastways not that I know of," I said. "And I don't much care what he thinks of Negros, you're coming over for dinner anyway. And sleepover too," I added stubbornly, mentally daring my dad to say no.

"So he doesn't know we're Negros?" Rocky asked incredulously.

"No and he's not *gonna* know until you walk through that door. And by that time it's gonna be too late because he's a polite southern gentleman and he don't just kick no one out that's been invited over to his house for supper, so that's all she wrote."

Rocky's face was still a combination of skeptical and terrified. "What if he throws us out? What if he tries to lick us? What if he invites his friends over and they hold a Klan meeting and try to hang us? This don't sound good at all. I don't believe you've thought this thing through, Val. I think we better not come."

"But you *gotta* come," I said. "Look, my dad ain't in the Klan. And he ain't a completely bad person. He's just kinda slow."

"Slow up here, you mean?" Rocky pointed to his head before grabbing another snickerdoodle.

"Slow up here, slow all kindsa ways. So if you come over and he gets to know you, not as 'Negroes' but as *people*—"

"Hang on," Rocky said. "You just hang on there, buddy boy." He had recently seen a movie where they said "buddy boy" a lot and now said it every chance he got. "It's not our family's job to teach your damn dad not to be prejudiced."

"He's not prejudiced, just stupid," I protested.

"Well, it's not our job to teach him how not to be *stupid,* neither! Look, we don't got no easy life. My dad could be taken away anytime, or someone could kill him by setting our house on fire. We live in that world every day so why would we make our life harder by coming over to your house just to teach your dad a lesson? That don't make no sense."

"I told you my dad ain't really evil."

"You said he *hates* Negroes! Your word, not mine!"

"Well, I might have been exaggerating a little bit there. He just thinks they should know their place—"

"Them's fighting words."

"Yeah they are, and I'll fight my dad if he says 'em in front of you. And if he even raises a little pinky to hurt you I'll grab our fire poker and shove it right up his ass," I said, amazed at my own language. I changed tack, my voice becoming soft and pleading and my eyes going gooey. "Look. You're my friend and so is your family. It's my house as much as my dad's and I want you guys to feel welcome there. I'm not trying to prove nothin' to nobody, I'm just trying to have my buddy over for dinner. You can come or you can not come," I said with a catch in my throat, trying not to sound too hurt. "In the long run, it don't matter none, I guess. But we *picked* each other to be friends. That means a lot more than some guy who just happened to borned me," I concluded, like a lawyer wrapping up a particularly airtight argument.

"I'll think about it," Rocky said after a pause.

"Hey," Rae-Rae called from behind the counter. "You two been sitting there long enough. You're driving all my other customers away."

"We're just eating snickerdoodles," I said. "We bought 'em here, and now we're eating 'em here."

"That was a damn hour ago," Rae-Rae said. "You're driving away business. Wrap it up and go somewhere else." She took a closer look at Rocky, whose stomach was looking a little flatter than usual. "You hungry, boy?"

"No, ma'am."

"Wait here." She went behind the counter, disappeared into the kitchen, and came back with a chicken salad sandwich with all the trimmings wrapped in wax paper. She gave half to Rocky and the other half to me. "If anyone asks, you brought these from home," she said. "Now go on, git."

So we got.

#

I went back to Rae-Rae's bakery by myself the next day. I was a little ticked off and frankly prepared for the worst. More than anything else I wanted her to apologize. That's a pretty awful thing to do, just throw kids out of your donut shop when most of the other seats are empty, and it was pretty obvious she was doing it because Rocky was a Negro. She was busy making the morning's biscuits when I caught her. She didn't even look up, but she must have recognized the rhythm of my footsteps or something because she said "Morning, *Val*," real cold like, adding "what can I do for you?"

"I don't want any cookies today, Rae-Rae," I said. "I just wanted to talk to you about what happened yesterday."

"Don't you ever learn?" she asked. "Do I have to *beat* sense into you? People don't want to see you with that... Rocky boy in my shop. It's not about what *I* think, it's about what *they* think."

"Is that so?" I challenged. "I didn't see none of them coming up to me to talk about who can sit in a cafe and who can't, and who can be my friend and who can't. *Ma'am*," I added pointedly. I was just about at my wit's end.

"Come back here," said Rae-Rae. "I want to show you something." She lifted up the counter gate so I could walk into the back of the store where she baked the cookies and biscuits. I made my skeptical face, but walked in anyway. She took me straight to the back, keeping a sharp eye on the front door in case a customer should wander in early.

"Back here," she said, "is where I bake all my goodies. I don't let nobody come in here except employees, so you should feel honored. It was Mr. Rae-Rae who used to be in charge of the baking, but since he up and died, it's all me. But I can't do it alone. I have to employ someone who knows the finer points, an expert who understands the *science* of baking and the *art* of baking, and every person I have ever employed to work back here has been a Negro. Now, just what does that say to you?"

"It says that you don't want to pay them much," I said. I wasn't trying to be smart or nothing. That just seemed like the obvious logical answer to my brain.

"Well, you're wrong," Rae-Rae replied. She lowered both the tone and pitch of her voice. "What it says is that change comes slowly. It requires patience. You have to get people used to new ideas."

"No change in this world ever happens unless people are impatient," I countered. "*Very* impatient, and I am the living proof."

Rae-Rae looked puzzled. "How's that, hon?" she asked, like she was asking a kindergartner what he wanted to be when he grew up.

"When my mama passed away," and I crossed myself here, "they wanted to take me away from my daddy. They wanted to send me away to a foster care home, with a stranger that I didn't even know. They had me meet with her, but she was a mean lady. She was smiling but I could tell through her smile that she was evil, and she would beat me within an inch of my life and pull my hair and yell and scream my face off all the time and just treat me real, real bad. And so I would not budge. I told the judge and the sheriffs and the child protection people that I wanted to stay with my daddy where I belonged, and I was *not* patient. I cried at the top of my lungs, real tears, not even fake ones, and I screamed and screamed and screamed until finally they let me stay with my daddy."

Rae-Rae's eyes got as big as her snickerdoodles for about a fraction of a second, and then her face went back to its normal self. "You're gonna go far, Val," she said. "I can't even tell if that story's real or if you just made it up here on the spot."

"If you believed it," I replied without smiling, "it don't matter." And we just looked at each other for the longest time, like two football players who all of a sudden discovered they were playing on the same team.

#

My father's experience with people of color had been mixed at best. He had lived in Mississippi all his life and was constantly griping about how it wasn't what it used to be. He frequently griped about Negroes acing him out of jobs—he did odd work, from longshoreman to night watchman—and, as with children, believed southern society was best served when they were seen and not heard. While his tone wasn't one of active hatred or even disdain, he went along with the rules, which contrary to what I told Rocky means he was prejudiced by default.

My dad was also lazy, and a slow learner, and drunk more often than sober. Any of those three things would have been bad by itself, but together they were a deadly combination. He became a drifter, able to put food on the table, but just barely, and to top it all off he had to endure the initial indignity of cooking the little food he brought home. He deftly turned this embarrassment into a point of pride, often showing off his latest creation to me and whatever lady friend he'd managed to snag that afternoon from the Spot, where 2 pm drinking was not only encouraged but mandatory. He was charming and fast with a story, and ladies often glommed onto him without the least thought about his future or, indeed, his past.

I have to admit I wasn't exactly relishing the moment when dad met Rocky, but we'd weathered a lot of troubles together since mom had died and I was confident we'd get through this one too. At the very least I was sure he'd be polite while Rocky was in the house, and if he did explode at me it would only be after Rocky was out the door, safely out of hearing distance with a good pork chop dinner weighing down his stomach.

That night, tossing and turning in bed, I got to wondering how it was that Dad had come to be so set in his ways. Surely someone had had to cut *him* a break at some point, though I couldn't figure out why they would. The truth was that life had always come pretty easily to him without even trying, like beginner's luck at fishing—at least from what he'd told me. He'd had his pick of more or less everything, with plenty of chances to mess up and be forgiven. Because of this, he lived in a sort of imaginary dimension, where he believed everyone else had the same shot at success and ability to bounce back from mistakes that he did.

I couldn't sleep and decided to make myself a bacon sandwich on white bread. Sometimes I made a BLT, if we had lettuce and tomato around the house. Other times I just made a straight bacon sandwich, and that was good too. I'd been cooking for myself for a couple of years. I'd seen dad do it and figured if someone of his limited brainpower could pull it off, I could at least give it a try. I took the paper-wrapped rasher out of the ice box (we didn't have an electric fridge), peeled a few strips of meat off it, and laid them carefully in a cast iron pan, working slowly to cut down on tearing. I turned on the gas and lit the flame with a kitchen match, then turned the flame up, just barely, so the bacon would render instead of burning.

"Bacon sandwich, eh?" my dad said, strolling into the kitchen nonchalantly. I should have known he would smell the unmistakable aroma of pork and applewood.

"Yep," I said.

"Make me one too, son?"

"Sure." I crowded a little more bacon into the pan and, just temporarily, let the flame out a notch higher. The grease crackled a little as the cooler bacon hit it.

There wasn't much to do but hang around, pace, and wait for the bacon to cook. I knew dad was going to want to make conversation, which he eventually did. He just wasn't that comfortable with silence.

"Can I talk to you in the living room?" he said.

"Sure, I guess." I glanced at the bacon to make sure it was on the lowest possible setting, and adjusted the pieces a little with a fork so they'd get done evenly. We moseyed over to the couch and sat down, eyeing each other warily.

"Why here and not the kitchen table?"

"Kitchen table's for informal chats, how-was your day kinda chats," he said. "Living room's for serious father-son discussions, and that's what this is."

"Oh." I could feel my shoulders knotting up and rising up above my ears. "This isn't about girls, is it? I already learned about that from Lance and Larry." My two oldest acquaintances, they had a year on me and were a little more street-smart.

"No, this ain't about girls," my dad said. "It's about me. I ain't gonna be around forever, Val. Any day now I could have a heart attack, or get run over by a bus, or get shot at by some ornery cuss at the Spot for no good reason at all. I want you to have a plan so when that happens you have a place to go. I ain't really got no family to speak of and no friends neither. Tell me right now, if something was to happen to me, where would you go?"

"Well, I—I don't rightly know."

"That's kind of my point. You *should* know. How about Miss Jeannie down the block? She seems to have taken a liking to you, and she's got two sons."

"I know. They pick on me every chance they get."

"Well, you gotta toughen up then! You can't let a little thing like that get in the way of a good home life." The bacon was beginning to smell delicious and I wondered how much longer my dad was going to keep torturing me with grown-up planning before I could finish making my sandwich and eat it. "How about Betty Sue Becker? She's a widow, she could use someone to look after."

"She smells like cat poop," I said.

"All right, she smells like cat poop," my dad agreed heartily. "But son, you got to stop being so picky. Otherwise if something happens to me the county will take over and they're not picky at all. They'll place you with any family wants you, and that's if you're lucky. I'd hate to see you have a hard life just because I had a losing streak."

"Dad, are you..." I couldn't find the words. "Are you *planning* something?" I smiled to indicate I was making a half-joke. But I wasn't laughing and neither was he.

"I owe a few people some money down at the Spot," he said finally. "Cards, horses, stuff like that. Nothing's big by itself, but together they kind of add up, and I can't pay anything back on the salary I make. So yeah, my days might be numbered. I'm just trying to plan for the future."

I started to get up so I could snuff the flame under the bacon or at least turn the meat. The air was beginning to fill with a dark smell that signaled the end of rendering and the beginning of burning. I was starting to lose my appetite for a bacon sandwich and really just wanted to follow basic safety at this point. "Sit down!" my dad said. "I ain't done talkin' yet." So I did, reluctantly.

The bacon smelled nastier and nastier. I began to detect, not just regular frying aromas, but nasty, choking, burning smoke. Meanwhile dad went right on talking. He himself smoked, and I think it might have affected his sense of smell.

"I ain't been the best father to you, Val," he said. "I know that. I work enough to feed you and I make you dinner every night and I listen to your stories from school and the little games you and your friends make up and the adventures you have. But I ain't taught you as much as I could and I ain't made you into as much of a man as I could. Don't think I don't know that. And I'm—I've tried to be there for you. That's about the most I can do."

"That's more than a lot of fathers do," I said, "and anyway, ain't no rush. I'll get there when I get there." I put my arm around him and gave him a comforting hug, and he gave me a vaguely sheepish look in return. I felt an odd urge to give him a teddy bear or some marbles to play with.

The transformation from delicious meat to noxious, putrid black cloud was now complete. It was impossible to ignore, even for someone as oblivious as my father, who soon began choking and gagging. Coughing up a storm myself but trying to stay low and dodge the smoke, I made my way into the kitchen where the grease fire was in full swing, with flames leaping so high I couldn't even see the tiny charred specks that used to be meat.

My father was close behind. "I'll get it," he proclaimed with great chivalry, rushing up to the water tap and filling up the coffee percolator.

"No, dad!" I said, knowing even at age 11 that water and hot burning grease didn't mix.

"It's OK," he said. "I used to be a volunteer fireman." Which had been true, for about two days; but all he'd done was hang out at the firehouse, play bingo, and eat chili.

As soon as the water from the percolator hit the grease, that was it. Fire splashed everywhere and if you've never seen fire splashing, I hope you never do. Then it was a short jump to everything in the house turning into an evil orange dance, from the grease-covered kitchen walls to the cheap plywood cabinets to the boxes of cornflakes Dad liked to leave lying around the newfangled nylon living room carpet. Everything went up and no stopping it.

I grabbed a knife that happened to be lying out on the counter and cut a big slash in the kitchen back screen door, yanked out a big piece of screen with my hand, and crawled out to safety, coughing and hacking all the way. I made my way around to the front yard and fully expected my dad to join me there, chastened but at least alive.

After a couple of minutes, when he didn't show up, I felt

compelled to go check on him. I was no hero, so when I peeked around the fence and saw that nothing but flame were visible in the kitchen, just a wall of orange and a noise like a million palmetto bugs chomping on something, I had to go to plan B.

I raced five houses down to where Rocky lived. I pounded on the door and rang the doorbell a bunch of times and yelled "Help!" until finally someone answered the door. It had to be Rocky's dad, though I'd never met him before. He was darker than Rocky and about 20 years older and a whole lot grouchier. A little prematurely gray hair was a sign he hadn't had an easy slide, and his narrowed eyes told me the last thing he wanted was a skinny, squeaky-voiced little white kid pounding on his door at one in the morning.

"What's going on?" he said. "Who are you?"

I explained to him that my house down the street was on fire and my dad was stuck in it. That was all I needed to say. Grimly, he ran in the direction of my pointed finger. I tagged along after, as fast as I could, partly because I knew seeing a Negro running down the street in his pajamas in the middle of the night would be enough reason for a lot of people to call the police.

When we came to my house, he didn't have to ask. Flames were visible coming out of the roof as well as a couple of the windows. Mr. Jordan went around the back way, peeked in the kitchen, took a very deep breath and then, holding it, reached in and dragged my dad out by the wrists, making the screen door hole about twice as big in the process. Mr. Jordan was a large man —half again as tall as my dad and much stronger—so it didn't surprise me that he was able to drag him out in one fell swoop. What did surprise me was that my dad, in spite of everything, appeared to be alive—barely.

"Who are you?" he said, demanding but also weary.

"I'm your neighbor," Mr. Jordan said, "and I just saved your life."

"No you didn't," my dad said without missing a beat. "I'm not gonna make it another hour."

"We'll get you to the hospital," Mr. Jordan said gruffly. "You're gonna be fine."

"I have a collapsed lung," my dad proclaimed.

"Dad, say thank you."

"I'm not thanking nobody," said my dad stubbornly, "because I'm not gonna make it."

"Dad," I said, "remember I was telling you about my friend Rocky? This is his dad."

"Yeah, I remember, Val."

"*You're* Val?" said Mr. Jordan. "*You're* the Val Rocky's always talking about?"

"He didn't tell you I was white, huh," I said, a little ashamed for no reason I could pinpoint.

"You didn't tell me Rocky was a negro, neither," my dad said accusingly.

"Dad," I said, "if anything happens to you, I'd like to stay with Rocky and his dad. Would that be OK with you?"

"Who said it was OK with *me*?" Rocky's dad asked, as our house went with a whoosh from being on fire but savable to being a lost cause whose yellow-orange beacon and black smoke could be seen from a mile away down the road. Sure enough, at that exact moment the volunteer fire department arrived in their clanging little red toy fire engine, acting all big and important.

"You move in with that man," my dad said, "and you are no son of mine."

And then he closed his eyes, and sure enough that was the last breath he ever breathed. Goddamn if he didn't think being right was more important than being alive.

#

I guess you know what happened after that. I moved in with Rocky and Mr. Jordan and Mrs. Jordan. Yes, there is a Mrs. Jordan, if you're wondering. She's a very nice lady, but I'd be glad to have even a mean lady in my life at this point. It's just nice to have a mom. My dad was a great dad, even if he was stupid and pigheaded, but Mrs. Jordan gives me big hugs and says reassuring things if I fall off my bike or get into a scrap with bullies. You know, mom stuff.

At first I thought it would be weird living with a Negro family, and in fact one time a couple of men from the sheriff's came and tried to take me away, saying the Jordans had no business with me and that they stole me and a bunch of other lies. But Mr. Jordan said he knew his legal rights and if they didn't have a warrant then they could come back when they did, and that he and his wife were just as qualified to raise me as anyone and considering they'd been together for 10 years probably more qualified than most. And that was kind of the end of that.

I never did get to have dinner with my dad and Jordan together. I sometimes wonder what it would have been like. I like to think that, after the initial shock, they would have gotten along pretty well. At the very least they would have respected each other. And they both liked to build balsa wood model airplanes, so they would have had something to talk about with each other. I think about that night pretty often, actually. In my mind I call it the Night that Never Happened.

Rocky and I still get along pretty good. We go fishing together down at the creek, and Rocky once caught two tiny frogs. We named them Abbott and Costello, and keep them in a big pickle jar with holes punched in the lid. Mr. Jordan showed me how to bait a hook, and how to reel a fish in slowly so you let him wear himself out, and a lot of other stuff my dad was too tired or drunk to teach me.

I've asked Mr. Jordan about the fire and how he rescued my dad a bunch of times, but he says he's no hero and anyway it was too little too late because my dad's dead. I guess he's right, you can't bring someone back from the grave. I think he feels bad about the whole thing because he failed, even though a lot of people wouldn't even have tried.

It's complicated, I guess. Mr. Jordan told me about some Chinese rule that if you save a person's life you're responsible for it from then on, and I told him that technically he didn't save my dad's life because he died the same night he was rescued from the fire. Or mine, because I knew enough to save myself.

We go back and forth on that a lot. Mr. Jordan is basically a person with the world on his shoulders and probably always will be.

I think things are getting a little nervous around town. I can understand why Mr. Jordan looks worried. When I go downtown with him or Mrs. Jordan, we get looks and then people look away and pretend they weren't looking at all. The only ones who just stare are police and sheriffs. They give me a really funny look like I'm a Martian or something. But they can't figure out what to do with me so they just leave me alone, at least for now.

I do have to use Negro bathrooms and Negro water fountains and eat at the Negro lunch counter and not only do I accept that, I like it. I'm basically a Negro as far as everyone in town is concerned and that's just fine with me.

My dad did not die for nothing.

6 A LITTLE BIRD

SLIDE #1

Benedetto stares into his coffee cup. VJ Day was one week ago and now he has been released from duty. He has no sweetheart, no real family, no hometown in fact having moved around for most of his life—rootless, and he likes it that way. Where should he go, what should he do? He's heard rumors of a postwar boom and wants to be in on it. The same way he was in on the Company D poker racket, the pony racket, the greyhound racket, the betting-on-all-the-other-rackets racket. He watches the sugar and cream swirl around in the coffee, making a beautiful hypnotic design until it's all one uniform gray-brown.

He doesn't know exactly what he's going to do, but he's going to do a lot of it.

SLIDE #2

What does Benedetto know how to do? Correction, he *thinks* he knows how to do a lot of things, but what does he *know* he knows how to do? Answer: he knows how to carry things. So he applies as a longshoreman. From there, he figures, it's a natural progression to head longshoreman, head of the San Francisco branch, maybe head of the company. Lifetime employment, what a great invention, he thinks. Security just like in the military, but in the private sector. Of course these companies make millions and even billions of dollars. Why shouldn't they give back to their communities that host them, by providing some stability and opportunity? It's a natural—a civilized plan from which his children and grandchildren will doubtless benefit.

Benedetto knows he looks spiffy in his new suit, even though it's straight off the rack. He'd woken up early enough to have a bath; shaved with a fresh blade and a mug full of brand new bay rum shaving soap; put some of that newfangled greaseless dressing in his hair, the one that smells like gasoline; and drank an entire pot of coffee. If anyone was ready for a job interview, it was him.

Benedetto practices his answers. "Yes sir... I was a turret man in the Navy, sir. With great power comes great responsibility, sir." Mostly he practices not having an accent. Benedetto began consciously losing his native intonation at five and by eight or nine had lost almost all of it; but every once in a while, it creeps back into the picture and he has to work to root it out, like a weed that won't go away. He mumbles these questions, and his answers, over and over to himself while in a long employment line, his form filled out half an hour before everyone else's. No question, the job is in the bag. He keeps on muttering his practice phrases, and some queers shoot him looks; but when he glares back, to show them he's serious and that messing with this particular Italian would be a huge mistake, they leave him alone.

He gets to the desk and surprise! The individual interviewing him is a woman. Well, he can charm the socks off the ladies and has frequently does, literally. Clearly this woman was hired, as many were, to fill a void after the office men had gone off to Europe or Japan to fight the war. An enchanting pale, buxom redhead with a few freckles and a turned-up nose, she is just his type: too naive to be suspicious, too clearly experienced to be truly innocent.

"We're full up on longshoremen," she tells him in the office. "We could use somebody, but it's for a different position. We need a *real man* for the job. Know any?" she adds insinuatingly.

"I'll do," Benedetto replies.

"You'll do *what?*" She doesn't wait for an answer. She stamps his application hard with a big, heavy wooden rubber stamp, so thick it's almost the size of her arm. I'd like to stamp *her* the way she just stamped my application, Benedetto thinks.

"Congratulations, you got the job."

"Thanks." Then: "What job did I get?"

"You'll find out."

To Benedetto, this is a satisfactory answer for now. The job is bound to pay a union wage, be based on the Embarcadero where lady pickings are easy, and have a well-trod path to a nice cozy future. What more does he need to know?

SLIDE #3

This job is for the birds. No, not just a silly, meaningless task not worth doing. It's *literally* for the birds—the canaries, parrots, parakeets, and budgies sold every day at Woolworth's variety at Market and Powell. Benedetto's job is to haul them safely from the pier, where they arrive from parts unknown, mostly South America, to the pet department, where willing buyers await. He checks in every day with the boss lady who hired him, whose real name is Radnitzky but whom he just calls Red, and who doesn't seem to be quitting or going anywhere. Then he escorts a shipment of birds down from the foot of Market, and back again. For these highly intellectual labors he gets paid a dollar an hour, with overtime on the weekends if he doesn't mouth off too much.

Benedetto is starting to enjoy the company of birds more than people. His fellow soldiers had constantly teased him for being Italian, for being short, for being a slob, for being a fop, for eating too much, for not eating enough, for eating foreign-looking foods, for being too much of a ladies' man and hence unmanly (he never could figure that one out), for kissing up to commanding officers, and for subordination that got the whole platoon on KP duty.

Benedetto often talks to his birds on the way to Woolworth's. "Lovely morning, Mr. Canary." "Looks like rain, Mrs. Budgie." "How do, Mr. Parrot? How's the wife and little ones." He enjoys these chats.

There's only one problem with this bird shipping job and that's that Benedetto believes he might be going a little bit nuts.

Let's face it, birds aren't the most communicative of creatures. And when they do communicate, they tend to whistle rather than talk, which is not helpful. Benedetto sometimes thinks he himself is turning into a bird. He begins preening himself by running a licked finger over his hair, whistling for buses and taxicabs, chirping little tunes when he's lonely or bored ("These Foolish Things Remind Me of You" being a favorite), flapping his arms like wings to keep them loose and limber when he thinks no one's looking. He realizes all this is happening, since he's fairly bright and self-aware. But he also realizes that human beings never did him any favors, just like some people fighting in the army alongside him who claimed that Roosevelt never stuck out his neck for them. Maybe now would be a good time to switch loyalties, side with his new avian friends.

One day as Benedetto is carting a crate of birds, by hand dolly, to the Powell-and-Market Woolworths, the inevitable happens. It starts talking to him.

"Good morning, Benedetto."

Benedetto looks around. There are people around, of course—it's Market Street—but no one appears to be addressing him. Certainly no one is looking at him.

He'd gone out to Mike's Tavern last night and had a few too many boilermakers. Must be hung over. Yes, that must be it. He clearly must be seeing pink elephants, or in his case hearing them. He knocks himself in the head a couple of times, yanks on his earlobes to help loosen the wax in his ears, so on. The other possibility is that there are a lot of Italians in San Francisco. Maybe one of them was calling another one and the name was vaguely like Benedetto: Gepetto, say, or Cornetto, or maybe even Gelato.

"I said good *morning*, Benedetto. What kind of whore was your mother to raise you like that, you don't even give a 'good morning' the time of day?"

"Bastard! Don't talk about my mother that way."

"Ha. Madeja talk."

"Who is this?" By now Benedetto didn't merely think he was going crazy, he was sure of it.

"Let me out and I'll show you."

"I'm wise to your little game. If I let you out, you'll fly away." Benedetto couldn't believe what he was saying, or who—what—he was saying it *to*, but he thought it important to make himself crystal clear all the same.

"I won't, I swear it on my mother's grave."

Benedetto grimaced, whipped out his pocket knife, and began to pry off the crate's lid, standing the dolly on its flat bottom to gain some leverage. Gawkers were many and helpers were none. The wood was solid pine at least an inch thick, held together by nine-penny nails that seemed to have been driven in by a machine rather than a man. Tweets of consternation came from within the crate, apparently from all the other birds that had not somehow suddenly gained a human voice, and those tweets were magnified and echoed by all the other birds on Market Street, the pigeons, the occasional seagulls in from the Embarcadero to scavenge the remains of a sandwich, the sparrows and jays who lived in the trees and woke up any winos, bums, and passed-out businessmen remaining on the streets with morning songs fresh and loud as the calls of donut vendors.

When Benedetto finally managed to get the case open, he held his hand against the needle-narrow slot, as a kind of makeshift perch, and out popped a tiny yellow head with a red stripe from neck to beak. A canary, surely, but of a kind Benedetto had never seen in his life. The red stripe on the head was a giveaway that this was a strange bird of unusual origin.

"Thank you," said the bird. "That was a little more polite than ignoring my 'good morning.'"

"Who are you," said Benedetto, as terrified as if a Martian had come down from space in a flying saucer and pointed a disintegrating gun at his head, "and what do you want?"

"Let's go somewhere safe," said the bird, "and I'll tell you."

SLIDE #4

The Woolworth's soda fountain probably wasn't the safest place for a bird. Prominently featured on the menu were products of violence against poultry: a turkey club sandwich, a chicken salad sandwich, an egg salad sandwich, and a two-piece serving of fried chicken. When Mr. Twitters (for that was apparently his name) pointed this out, he was greeted by Benedetto's large, coarse tongue sticking out at him right before Benedetto took a nice healthy bite out of his turkey club.

"This is a key period in American history," Mr. Twitters said. "Human history, in fact. I need you to play your part. Don't let me down."

"Are you nuts?" Benedetto said. "Do you want to join your friends over there in the pet department? There's a cage waiting over there with your name on it. Look, I was a turret jockey. I almost got my ass blown up five or six times, and that's on top of having to eat disgusting MRE's every day and getting mercilessly beat on by bigger sailors. And let's not even get into the sex."

"No, let's not," Mr. Twitters agreed.

"So I think I've earned the right to do whatever I please with my life, and not listen to a stranger who happens to think I need to take part in some all-important secret mission and is, not for nothing, a *bird.* You're a psychotic voice in my head. There is every reason in the world why I should not listen to you, at all, ever." And to emphasize his point, he put his hands over his ears. "La la la la. La la la la." The other diners at the lunch counter all swiveled their heads around and looked in the crazy man's direction, their mouths dripping gravy and cottage cheese.

"Don't listen to me," said Mr. Twitters, "and you risk ruining everything for everybody."

Benedetto took another bite of his sandwich. He was enjoying it, particularly the turkey, which was melt-in-his-mouth tender in the way that a delicious bird, so plump it could barely fly and raised entirely for his own personal delectation, should be.

"I'm listening," he said.

SLIDE #5

A gum-popping waitress with hair styled into rolls like telephone cable coils on either side of her head, and a third in the front, stared at Benedetto as he held his little bird pow-wow over his empty sandwich plate. Takes all kinds, she thought. Sally down in Pets must be desperate for birds, to have jokers like this deliver them.

"This is a very prosperous time, and it's going to get more prosperous for a while—more than you can dream of, some years," Mr. Twitters opined. "All that prosperity's going to look great to people who grew up in the depression. But it's going to come at a cost. Factories and plants are going to pump disgusting waste into rivers, lakes, oceans, and streams, killing fish as well as nearby birds and ultimately making it impossible for any but the simplest living things to survive. Mankind will suffocate itself."

"You're not making any sense. California's still mostly open space and so is most of the west, even the middle west from what I understand. And you're saying a few factories are going to change all that? What's your advice? Close them down so no one has a job, I suppose? Send all the men back to the army?"

"Listen or don't," Mr. Twitters shot back. "I'll be long dead before any of this happens. You'll have children and grandchildren and you'll see it affect them. And," he added, "it will break your heart."

"Go to hell," said Benedetto. He pushed his plate away and put a dollar and a half next to it, including a dime tip—much more than such a nosy waitress deserved, he thought. He lit a Lucky and immediately trundled over to Pets to leave Mr. Twitters with Sally. He'd claim he'd made a mistake just left one out—that was all. No harm done.

Benedetto had had enough problems with his conscience and the past. He'd torpedo-blasted plenty of Japs, many of whom had probably homes and families. He didn't need any conscience problems with the future.

SLIDE #6

Benedetto, that night, trying to pick up on a girl in a bar. She's a hot number, all right, dolled up in a skintight green satin dress and high heels with her hair styled to look like Rita Hayworth's, or maybe Veronica Lake's. Her name is Carol. She's pounding shots like there's no tomorrow, not grasshoppers or pink squirrels, mind you, but *shots,* with a speed and relish Benedetto associated only with men and lesbians; but she was looking his way, no denying it. He's hunched over yet another boilermaker and trying to forget his troubles, which mostly consist of being crazy enough to talk to birds, birds who converse not in regular small talk mind you but in scary, paranoid scenarios of the kind science fiction writers are paid to dream up. No thank you.

He offers her a hand when the band strikes up the next number, a peppy rhumba, and they cut a rug around every other dancer on the floor. Bendetto's mama had been a dance contest champion and had taught him some moves, right before she ran away with the milkman.

"Are you from around here?" Benedetto asks, by way of making conversation. He figures if he can hold her for an hour or so, she's his and then they can sneak off somewhere private, like his flat or her mother's house if there's a thick bedroom door.

"What a silly question." She removes a glove with her teeth, biting the index finger hard for emphasis. "Nobody's from around here. People come here from all over the world. This isn't where you come from, it's where you come *to.* It's where you come to escape husbands, bullies, drunks, people who want to treat you like a 'little lady,' people who want to slap your ass while you percolate the coffee and fix the bacon and eggs, people who beat you at night and apologize in the morning."

"Sounds like the voice of experience."

"Sorry I can't be more lighthearted and gay. It's kind of a sore point with me." She removes her other glove, same way as the first one. "I don't understand why people like... *him* make life so hard for people like me, but they do. Anyway, I'm here now." She primped her hair. "And so are you..." She stared at him with big green eyes that she was quite clearly making bigger and greener on purpose.

"Do you want to go somewhere?" Benedetto said. He said it out of habit—it *felt* like the right move to make and the right time to make it. "Somewhere quiet where we can get to know each other better, just you and me? Maybe a coffee shop where we can put something in our stomachs besides cocktails?"

"Sure, champ," Carole says, giving him a not-particularly-innocent punch in the shoulder. She's clearly drunk as a skunk; in fact the bartender at this place is famous for making up "dare drinks" like tonight's Snooty Skunk, one part Black and White Scotch, one part fresh cream and one part licorice schnapps, as disgusting to drink as it is to say. So she ought to be easy pickings, and that's exactly what Benedetto is planning to do: pick her, like a ripe orange.

They get into his car, Carole's hands running all over him including his face, chest, and lap, and they end up skipping the cafe in favor of more intimate surroundings, i.e., her apartment. When they get there, he's stunned. The place is not only enormous but decorated with perfect taste, spare but not too spare with a hand-picked mix of Danish modern design and antiques. This broad is loaded, is the none too subtle message. The message is strengthened when she excuses herself to slip into something a little more comfortable and then comes back in a silk kimono bearing two glow-in-the-dark cocktails in space age-style glasses. She presses a single switch to dim the lights and turn on the hi-fi at the same time. This is the first time Benedetto has ever heard one of the new hi-fis, and he's stunned. It's everything he ever thought it would be, and then some. Every press of a piano key, every stroke of the violin bow rendered in searing detail as though he were right in front of the orchestra. He's mesmerized by the sound, and by Carol's cleavage under her flaming orange and yellow kimono.

"I'm hoping," Carol says as they toast, "that you won't mind getting right down to brass tacks. I'm a single woman living alone, and not shy about needing company now and again. But I'd like to know more about you. I know you're not bad looking, and muscular, and a fine dancer. But what do you do?"

"I ship exotic birds," Benedetto says truthfully.

"Exotic birds? Oh, how wonderful. You must live a daring and exciting life, traveling to South America and the South Sea Islands and parts unknown. You know," she says, lighting a cigarette from a table lighter with an enormous flame that nearly singes her hairdo, "I've always wanted to travel and those are exactly the places I've always wanted to travel *to.*" She draws nearer, puts an arm around Benedetto's head, and daringly finishes her entire drink in one swallow, casting the glass aside. Made of space-age resin, it bounces rather than shatters, leaving a trail of minute droplets. "And how are your prospects, if I may ask?"

"I'm actually well on my way to president of the company," Benedetto says, and it's true too. He's officially an independent contractor now, a freelancer paid on piecework, which means that he is in fact *already* president of the company—his *own* company in which he's not only president but janitor.

"This is all very exciting," Carol says. "Well, I'm not one to mince words so let's get right to it, shall we?" She locks and deadbolts the door and invites him to the bedroom with a come-hither finger, a steamy glance, all the greatest tunes in the Hit Parade.

Benedetto needs this. He's been alone and without physical human contact for too long. Does he sense that there is something too pat going on here, something so scripted and planned and clichéd that it should be wrapped in quotation marks from beginning to end? Sure he does. He's not *that* dense. But he also understands that he's a man and she's a woman, et cetera, et cetera. And she obviously wants to get laid, and as Benedetto typed on the typewriter that he bought from Woolworth's on trade credit, *Now is the Time for All Good Men to Come to the Aid of Their Party.*

#

Benedetto wakes up to find a note from Carol. In a hasty scrawl, it thanks him for a nice time and invites him to fix himself some breakfast. It also mentions that she has to hurry off to her important job as an Executive Secretary and absolutely cannot be late, thank you so much for understanding, and she hopes they'll get together again sometime soon.

He then looks around, and what does he see? On the floor, on the bedspread, on the dresser, covering the hi-fi out in the living room, licking the sugary inside of the empty space-cocktail glass.

Birds.

Not living birds, either. Dead birds. Decaying corpses of pigeons, seagulls starlings, sparrows, robins. And not just city birds. Ducks, geese, coots, loons, herons, red-tailed hawks and turkey vultures. Every bird that makes its home in the Bay Area is here, tits up and ready for the soup pot. I have no regrets, thinks Benedetto in regard to his latest one-night conquest. No, he doesn't but he does have *egrets,* right there on the floor, two of them, beaks pointed heavenward, waiting to be kidnapped into some flying Noah's Ark.

And there are more. Flamingos from Florida, penguins from the South Pole, jays from everywhere because there's no environment in which they don't thrive (and steal every other bird's food). The tiniest hummingbird and the most majestic bald eagle, there he is right there, a little mental version of "Taps" plays for him, the very symbol of our country dead on the floor like the noble ideals from which he sprang.

This can't be real, Benedetto thinks. This must be from something she put in the drink. I've finally gone over the edge, because this can't be happening.

He gets out of bed, thinking he'll splash his face with cold water from Carol's fancy silver plated Danish modern bathroom basin tap, and gets a footful of feathers and squish. Some tiny bones under his foot go *crunch.*

Oh, yes. It's real, all right.

He remembers the words of the canary who spoke to him so seriously, so tragically, in Cassandra-like tones about the unforeseen risks and dangers of progress and the precariousness of civilization.

He would like to wring that canary's neck.

SLIDE #7

Benedetto can't take anymore. He has no family and hates life too much to have friends. He has *colleagues*—colleagues who call him cheese-eater and dago and Luigi, colleagues who ask him in a Chico Marx-esque accent to hurry up and bring-a da fresh pizza pie and spaghetti with spicy meat-a-balls. His only escape is that he's a fine ladies' man, a charmer who can bed two, even three women in a single night as others look on with thinly disguised envy. And now what is shutting the whole operation down? A bird, a tiny bird that most people would love to adopt as their personal pet, a harmless thing barely capable of biting the head off a full-grown worm.

Sourly, Benedetto passes the appliance store on Market Street which has just got in a big new shipment of Philco televisions. He looks through the window at a row of seven TVs right out of Buck Rogers: clean, curvy, space-age lines, objects of lust for married men looking for electronic mistresses. And on those screens? All tuned to the same channel, the TVs create pinpoint matrix images, stripe after stripe with unrelenting authority, of a little yellow cartoon bird swinging on a little wooden swing, in a little wire cage. Harmless, harmless, harmless.

I tawt I taw a puddytat.

In inflamed rage, Benedetto spits at the window. The spit rolls down the glass in big viscous chunks, Benedetto having had cereal with cream for breakfast that morning. The store owner, a portly man with a shiny suit and a ruddy complexion, catches him in the act and runs out to the sidewalk with a scowl on his face the size of a Mack truck, half a jimmy-covered donut still in his hand.

"I don't know what you think you're doing, buddy," he says, "but I run a clean shop and I'm sick of bums and losers like you defacing public property. Why do you guys all hate America? I'm making a citizens' arrest." And so saying, he crams his hammy fist into Benedetto's eye, then his mouth, then his other eye, and finally his gut just to make a clean job of it.

"See how you commies like it," he says, showily dusting off his hands and stepping inside to make his call.

So Benedetto lies there, a pain in his gut like someone is trying to rub a bowling ball right through his stomach, face smashed, teeth aching, blood running warmly onto his chin and covering his hand when he goes to wipe his face.

A little bird told me, he thinks. I always wondered where that old saying came from. And he lies there in stunned, gelatinous silence until a cop comes by—the same cop, it soon becomes clear, that the appliance shop owner called for on the telephone.

"You anarchists think you know it all," says the cop. Benedetto appreciates the upgrade, or downgrade, from "communist" to "anarchist," but how can he tell the cop that neither label applies to him and that the reason, the *real* reason he spat on a strange store window was a Tweety Bird cartoon? Instead he just bows to the absurdity of the situation.

"I'm sorry, officer," he says. "I wasn't thinking and didn't really mean any harm. I'll cover the damages."

"There's no amount of money that will cover that *attitude*, Sonny Jim," the cop swipes. "The only thing now is to take you down to the station and book you. Defacing public property, willfully spreading disease, trespassing, disturbing the peace...there's a lot we can do with you and don't think I don't know it."

So they take Benedetto down to the station in the back of a paddy wagon, handcuffed and crying out in horrible pain.

"Don't be such a crybaby," says the cop. "You're worse than the kid I booked for shoplifting this morning. Anyway, it don't matter if you cry, 'cause your mommy and daddy ain't here to help you."

Everything goes hazy and woozy and dim and almost black from the blows, and then the little bird appears to him again. "This wouldn't have happened if you hadn't spent the night with that floozy," it says.

"What's that supposed to mean?" Benedetto has given up trying to figure out whether the bird were real or hallucinatory a long time ago. Now he's just going to judge it on the merits of what it's saying, or the lack thereof.

"It means that she's gonna have a baby. She'll try to get it taken care of in some back alley but that probably won't work. Then that baby's going to have other babies, and so on and so on and so on. All contributing to the explosion of the human species on this planet which will then result in the demise of all other species and probably humans themselves as well. And she's already pregnant and there's nothing you can do to stop it. The child is the progeny of two sex-hungry and hormone-crazed people so of course when it grows up there's every chance it's going to be just as sex-hungry and hormone-crazed, and have *more* children and *more* children and *more* children—"

"Do you not know when to shut up!" Benedetto snaps out loud at the bird, who gives him a shrug if birds can indeed be said to shrug. "Jesus, talk about poor timing. You're liable to get us both killed. Shut up, shut the hell up!"

Well, that's all the encouragement the cop needs. Thinking these ravings are meant for him, he stops the car, turns around, and beats Benedetto silly from the front seat, like he hadn't already had enough from the roughneck appliance salesman. He rocks Benedetto's jaw like a prizefighter, pulling all the way back so his elbow is hunched over the steering wheel, then springing forward in a powerhouse that practically knocks Benedetto's entire set of teeth out of his mouth. After that it's open season on Benedetto, mostly involving hard punches to the face. Benedetto could swear brass knuckles are involved as well, but it's hard to tell through all the horrible, relentless pain.

"It wasn't me," Benedetto mumbles through a broken jaw to the little yellow bird he sees still fluttering nearby, as he lies broken on the police car seat gazing up at the inside of the station wagon roof. "It wasn't my fault.... someone made me do it... not responsible... not my fault."

"That's what they all say," tweets the bird merrily.

SLIDE #8

Released on bail and more than slightly worse for wear, Benedetto takes the only path open to him, which is to see a psychiatrist. They're all the rage now, aren't they? There's one on every street corner. All the talk at parties is my analyst this, my analyst that, my analyst told me. And Benedetto must be crazy, since he keeps hearing and seeing something that cannot possibly be there. A hallucination, to call it exactly what it is. So, for him, a smart and non-superstitious mid-20th-century man (who goes to confession every Sunday because it's cheap insurance, but come *on*), there can be no other option.

True to form, the psychiatrist is a portly, bearded gent with big horn-rimmed glasses and an Austrian accent. His office sports the traditional couch, which Benedetto lies upon in the traditional manner.

"Zo," the psychiatrist says in his dulcet Austrian tones that go down like coffee and schwarzwaldkuchen, "how long haff you hated your muzzer?"

"I love my mother, you son of a bitch," adding, "them's fighting words."

"Mebbe zo," the shrink replies smoothly, "but sometimes fighting words are just what we need, ja? If there is no fighting, then there is no truth. Lying is easy but the truth is hard, ja?"

"Ja," Benedetto sulks. He's just glad his parole officer ante'd up for these sessions, since he can neither afford to pay for them himself nor would he ever do so.

"Ve are going to have to go vay, vay back into your childhood for this one," the shrink says. As Benedetto lies back staring at the ornate ceiling, he can hear the shrink biting off the end of a cigar and lighting it. Probably one of those really expensive ones, from his hourly rate. "Do you remember any birds zat you had as a child?"

"We had a parakeet once. We called it Farfalle," Benedetto lies. "We didn't know how to take care of it. It lasted all of four weeks. "

"Interesting. And who, perhaps, does this bird... *remind* you of?" the shrink asks accusingly, closing in for the kill. "Perhaps someone in your... *immediately family?* Someone who should have provided love and affection, but did not?"

"I dunno," says Benedetto, checking his watch.

"Now look here, Mr. Benedetto," the shrink proclaims, shooting an enormous H-bomb cloud of black smoke toward the ceiling. "Without cooperation we can achieve nussing. I assume you are not in therapy under duress."

"Well, I kind of am," Benedetto says. "The cops told me I would get locked up for six months unless I got myself a shrink. Six months of shrink or six months of pokey, that's what they told me."

"This guy's about as much of a shrink as I am," says the little bird, suddenly appearing on Benedetto's shoulder. "Are you going to let this phony, fake, ferkokter Freud push you around? Not only is he phony, he's *worse* than phony because people depend on him, trust in him. They tell him all their troubles and in return he takes their hard-earned $20 a session and tells them absolutely nothing, just nods and goes "mm-hm" and maybe, if they're lucky, every once in a while prescribes a primitive tranquilizer which has about the same effect as a shot of scotch except it doesn't taste as good. You know what I recommend you do with phonies like him? I recommend you put him out of his misery, so he doesn't have the opportunity to prolong anyone else's."

"I can't kill a shrink," says Benedetto, looking around drastically and frantically and, he has no doubt, suspiciously at the vaguely medical accouterments around the office: the leather-bound books with Latin on the spines, the glass jars full of cotton gauze, the plaques and diplomas with snakes wrapped around sticks. "It'll land me in prison, if not in a loony bin with a slice of rubber between my teeth while they fry my brain to bacon with hot electrodes."

"Look," says the bird, "I'm not asking you to be logical or rational here. I'm just asking you to be a good solid Joe."

"I thought you were all about protecting *life*," says Benedetto, feeling himself being swayed.

"True," says the bird, "but part of that is knowing when to quit, when someone's lived a good long life and can afford to give up the ghost."

"But - "

"Think," the bird went on, "of all the obnoxious, bratty children this man won't have, or the spoiled grandchildren. Extrapolate that twenty thousand years into the future and you could spare the Earth the burden of a thousand people! Or more! Then there are all the wasted hours you'll save the man's wannabe patients, people who should be discovering the secret of life not in talk therapy but in love, or a great meal or a beautiful sunset, and instead are compelled to spend an hour in this stuffy, smoke-filled office. *You* can relieve their suffering. *You* can relieve their pain."

If Benedetto had ever heard a more compelling argument, he couldn't think of when. And after all, he really had nothing to live for right now. No parents, no family, no love, no career. He pictured the Earth as the bird described it, thousands, perhaps millions of years from now, people dressed in space suits with fish bowl helmets, flying above the surface of the earth in their hovercrafts and buying the latest space appliances with their space money. He thought of how many people he would save from that overcrowded zoo of a planet by dissuading their forebears from seeing this charlatan.

A final thought—the thought of the beer he planned to have when it was all over—and Benedetto lunged at the shrink's good sharp wooden-handed letter opener, picked it up, and bade Dr. Fraud a fond but bloody adieu.

"Sometimes," he said, "a letter opener is just a letter opener."

SLIDE #9

And so Benedetto, like so many of his immigrant and son-of-immigrant and grandson-of-immigrant brethren at that point, was sent to prison on a charge of second-degree murder without malice aforethought. There hadn't been any malice during or after, either. Benedetto's little bird had simply warned him of the consequences of *not* acting—not consequences in a week or a year, but a thousand years from now. The fact that the bird hadn't been real didn't matter. Dr. Salzman had been found lying face down in a pool of his own blood on the floor of his own office. That *was* real, and no taking it back.

When Benedetto was inducted into prison, he somehow mysteriously found himself with a lot of other people of southern European extraction. Other Italians, yes, but also Greeks, Turks, Jews, Spanish, Armenians, and Southern French. There were even a few Poles and Romanians to spice things up. He was a little nonplussed by the racial mix. He had seen photos of similar scenes when they were released following WWII, the Nazis having kept them secret during the war itself, but never imagined being part of one. Regular white Americans, English, northern Europeans were nowhere to be found. Neither were Negroes or Orientals – they were in yet another prison system, Benedetto imagined, or at least a different section of this one.

"What you in for, man?" said the new inmate next to Benedetto, making friendly conversation. He had a greased-back pompadour and goatee. He seemed like a reasonable type, social but careful, with the slightly paranoid eyes of a man who's chosen a life of crime yet is a terrible liar and knows it.

"Murder," said Benedetto, as nonchalantly as possible. He'd known his whole life had been leading up to this, and now here he was. Everything he'd ever said or done had been pointing in this direction.

"Yeah, me too," said the beatnik. "You must have hated the son of a bitch, huh?"

"Nope," Benedetto said. "Only knew him for 50 minutes."

"You killed a stranger? Man, that's cold." The beatnik inched away from Benedetto surreptitiously. Sneakily, like he was trying not to piss him off. "Who was he?"

"Shrink."

"Why'd you kill him?"

Benedetto smiled. "A little bird told me to."

SLIDE #10

Here comes Carol to visit with Benedetto. It's not a conjugal visit exactly, since they're not married. But you wouldn't know that from the way Carol is dressed. She's wearing an emerald evening dress that's both backless and strapless, in broad daylight mind you. Over this rather risqué getup she wears a tan trenchcoat, the favorite of perverts and violators everywhere, hiding nothing and revealing everything. Finally, to complete the sleazy and fully questionable look, she wears a copper-red wig topped with a fedora.

"You really don't *need* to keep dressing that way to visit me here."

"What way?" Naively.

"You know. Like a moll."

"Is that still a word? Anyway, I feel more comfortable here when I dress this way." She hangs an unlit pastel-colored cigarette from the corner of her mouth, smoking being forbidden. "You know what other words you don't hear a lot these days?" she muses. "Fimble-famble. Hugger-mugger. Also, bootlegger. You don't hear that one much anymore."

"Why are you here?"

"I missed you," Carol says.

"I killed a man."

"You killed a psychiatrist, which is not the same thing." She runs a finger through her patently fake fishing-line curls. "Anyway, maybe I like tough guys. They're a challenge. Is there a place we can go?" She looks around. "I know we're not technically married, but maybe you can slip a guard a fiver to look the other way, or something."

Benedetto did not want any of this. Carol is used to dealing with criminals, he can tell, but he is not used to being one, and it's beginning to wear thin. He's not here because he's a tough guy. He's here because he's been talking to an imaginary animal who can see the future and advises him to kill now in order to save the human race later. It's a completely different concept.

Of course the old question is, if you had a time machine and could use it to go back in time to kill Hitler, would you do it? It's only been a few years since old Adolf offed himself, so the memory is still plenty fresh in everyone's minds. Benedetto ponders this conundrum as Carol chats up the guard. Certainly he would have saved millions of lives, but murder of any human is wrong and how do you know you wouldn't be able to talk him out of it? There's no easy answer.

Apparently there is an easy answer to gaining access to the conjugal visit area, though. Carol slips the guard a bill. He nods appreciatively, then winks and makes a comment clearly meant to be lewd, which she gamely laughs off. She motions to Benedetto to follow her, which he does, in his drab gray prison uniform that seems designed to show off his paunch and dull-razor 5 o'clock shadow.

"How long do you have left in here?" Carol says when they're in a partially clothing-optional clinch.

"Eight years, and that's if I get time off for good behavior. Considering that my behavior up until now hasn't been so swell, that's far from guaranteed."

"I miss you."

"Have you been faithful?"

"Don't make me laugh." She begins to give him the lowdown on each and every lover she's taken since he donned his prison stripes. They number in the low fifties, it seems, but she's very discreet and doesn't kiss and tell.

"I want you to know," she says, "that when you get out, I'm completely and totally yours." Then: "Why'dja do it, anyway?"

"I told you, a little bird came to me and it told me that we're ruining the world with too many people."

"A talking bird. Like a burning bush?"

"Something like that."

"That was a *hallucination*, you nitwit. Someone in the desert got too drunk and had too much sun, and they saw a mirage."

"That's one explanation," Benedetto says. "But I know what I know and I saw what I saw. It was as real as life. It was *more* real to me than anything in this place."

"Let me ask you something," says Carol, cheeks flushed. It's clear she's taken with him, but she refuses to let the issue go. "Are you Moses? Are you Jesus? Are you a character in a fairy tale? Or a myth or a fable? Is that what you are?"

"Carol, I - "

"No? Then I suggest you forget whatever it is that's telling you to do these things," she said, "so that when you're finally released, we can concentrate on living."

She gave Benedetto a big, passionate kiss. In spite of everything, she loved him. It felt strange to Benedetto, being able to do no wrong. His childhood sense of Catholic shame washed over him. Someone can see you while you're doing dirty things, he thought, and with a woman you're not even married to. He continued to think this while Carol continued to kiss him with waxy scarlet pillow lips, her foundation powder rubbing off on his face, its distinctive, overpowering scent in his nose mixing with the stale smoke from her hair.

"I have to go soon," she said. "We can't actually do anything because we're not married. But we can change that, if you want," she added hopefully and a little forlornly. "I asked, and the chaplain here is allowed to marry us. He's even allowed to do Catholic," she added, as though this somehow sealed the deal.

Benedetto was nonplussed. Marriage hadn't really been in his plans and definitely wasn't now. After all, what prospects did he have? He'd murdered a man, plus he was a nut job as far as everyone else knew—hell, as far as *he* knew.

"I love you," Carol said, her eyes growing wide and welling up.

"You too," Benedetto said as the guard stepped up, signaling that their time was over. He didn't ask them to separate. He didn't have to.

SLIDE #11

Well, time marched on. Benedetto was a model inmate, participating in all the new psychological plans for social improvement, programs designed to reintegrate the inmate into society while making him see the error of his ways and causing him to be productive rather than vindictive, et cetera, et cetera.

Benedetto's loner tendencies didn't exactly help him in prison, and further adding to his alienation was his tendency to make Cassandra-like pronouncements to anyone and everyone with whom he spoke. But the warden liked him, and the guards learned to joust with his dark sense of humor. Eventually he worked his way up to senior warehouse supervisor. He was in charge of things that got shipped into the prison, such as Spam and vegetables and new uniforms and cleaning supplies; and also of things that got shipped out of the prison, such as letters and crafts. He knew a fair amount about shipping and warehousing dating back from his longshoreman days, so the work was familiar and, it must be said, not mentally demanding. Some salt-and-pepper began peeking out from Benedetto's crew-cut hairline and he began to lose a little on top, and ventriloquist dummy lines began to form from his mouth to his chin; but he did his pushups and sit-ups in the gymnasium every day, and didn't age too badly.

Brezynski, the guard dropped by the library when things were slow. Today was one of those days. He and Benedetto talked sports, literature, whatever came to mind. They got on pretty well, although Brezynski never let him forget who was who.

"Did you see what that bastard Truman did?" said Brezynski. To him all politicians were bastards.

"It doesn't matter," Benedetto said, not even looking up. "There are too many people on this damn planet. It doesn't matter who's in charge of them. You'll figure that out one of these days. Gimme a bite," he said, motioning to Brezynski's donut.

"Gimme a smoke," Brezynski retorted, and they traded. Benedetto lit Brezynski up as he chowed down on Brezynski's frosted raised with rainbow sprinkles.

"How come inmates don't get donuts?" Benedetto said. He'd asked the same question about five thousand times.

"Health reasons," Brezynski replied. "Dr. B. says prisoners need to eat nutritious food."

"But guards don't?"

"I thought you were all for taking needless humans out of the population." Brezynski took a giant bite of donut. "Why should I eat a square meal like ham, bacon, eggs, and coffee with fresh cream when I can eat these deadly things?"

"You got me there," Benedetto said.

"I still think you're crazy," Brezynski opined. "There's plenty of room in the world for everybody, Americans and commies and Chinese and Arabs and Eskimos. Sure we're all trying to kill each other and blow each other up with H bombs and whatnot, but you can't just stop the human race. Progress is what makes the world go around. No progress, no donuts," he added. So saying, he devoured the last of his own pastry, whereupon he went pale. "I don't feel so good," he said, and clutched the left side of his chest. "I think I ate that a little too fast. You got any bromo?" And he collapsed to the ground.

Well, that was the end of Brezynski. Benedetto thought fast. All his life, he had been an opportunist out of necessity, but opportunities themselves had been few and far between. Now one was staring him right in the face. He looked around furtively to make sure there were no other guards around, but none was. The loading dock was guarded pretty lightly, especially in wintertime with the temperature dropping to minus 20 sometimes. The guards didn't go where they were needed, they went where it was comfortable, and if it was uncomfortable *and* they weren't needed they didn't touch it with a 10 foot pole. Benedetto yanked off Brezynski's uniform, being careful not to break the shirt buttons; doffed his own; and put it on instead. He put an ear to Brezynski's mouth and nose, just to make sure he wasn't still breathing; but no, he was a goner with an exclamation mark. Benedetto left Brezynski lying there in his skivvies, dodged out the loading dock door, and hopped into a waiting canoe. The ancient, greying wooden panels were already beginning to abrade his hands as he rowed off for San Francisco, not knowing where he was going to stay or how but only that he had to survive.

SLIDE #12

The crickets were almost loud enough to drown out Benedetto's thoughts as he constructed a makeshift lean-to in the Marin headlands. The sunset had been beautiful, but in Benedetto's mind it had been mocking him: his behavior, his lack of friends or family or place, the very notion that his life had value at all. Its reds were garish and gratuitously sexual, its yellows bilious, its oranges predatory like an enormous tiger threatening to bite off his head.

"Well, little bird," Benedetto said, "it's just me and you now. It won't be long before they catch us, and we'll get the chair for sure. That's if something doesn't happen to us in the meantime. Freezing to death in the rain, tripping on a rock and breaking a leg so we're left to starve or become turkey vulture meat, it all adds up to bad news."

There was no answer from the bird, who was apparently on

vacation. Benedetto hadn't seen or heard from him since he'd busted out. Maybe he really had made the whole thing up, after all —the hallucinatory product of a stressful life, no more real than a Napoleon hat-wearing maniac's delusions of grandeur, or the hophead's belief that he can fly right out a window.

Benedetto looked up at the sky. As the stars came into the kind of clear focus you only get when you leave the city, his eyes welled up. Who was he to have tempted fate? To think he was better than everyone else, above the law, beyond human instinct and desire? To live a life of shortsighted temperamentality, doing whatever he felt like without regard for the consequences?

Nobody, that's who.

Was he sorry? No. He'd done the best he could with what he had. If he wasn't a particularly steady guy, not a planner or a restrained, sane person, he'd just have to deal with the results.

A heavy rustle came from the brush, followed by some light footsteps in the leaves. Probably a large raccoon or a small deer. Benedetto's predatory instincts told him to go after this potential food source, but immediately afterwards, instincts that were now much more powerful told him NO. And so he lay there, in the fetal position, head in hands and knees curled toward his head, waiting like a rabbit.

Don't eat me, he thought. I'm not here.

SLIDE #13

Benedetto woke up to find himself oddly warm and comfortable when he opened his eyes. The first thing he saw was a gauzy, cottony whiteness, like being inside a ball of surgical cotton. *I must be dead*, he thought. *Well, it had to happen sooner or later.* He smelled the sharp odor of alcohol and the sly, insidious scent of Novocain.

As Benedetto came to, he realized that he was awake, relatively speaking. He tried to lift his arms to whip the sheet off his head and found that he was unable to do so, that his arms were in fact bound to his sides with what seemed to be rather strong, rough, fibrous rope.

Then the sheet was lifted off his head for him—slowly, cautiously, as though with a great, shaky struggle. As the smells of alcohol and Novocain became stronger, a minty, cinnamony toothpaste aroma was added to the mix. As the sheet fell to the floor drape by drape, an enormous rounded, yellow shape emerged from behind it. It couldn't be, Benedetto thought. And yet it was: Benedetto's yellow bird, tall and big around as the professional wrestlers from the TV Benedetto had sometimes glimpsed through his neighbor's window. Its face was large and impersonal, its eyes beady yet enormous, evil green light shining from them. It looked at Benedetto as though he were a delicious worm. Its beak seemed to be smiling, but it was a smirking, alligatorish smile, not a sign of happiness or contentment.

"I thought you were my friend," say Benedetto, realizing too late that maybe this was a dream after all, but not a good one.

The bird, who's not talking today, responds by flapping his wings. It is an enormous flap, revealing a wingspan of nine or 10 feet, all of them covered in brilliant yellow feathers. Its gaze is unblinking and Benedetto's feeling is that it would just as soon eat him as help him. It is by far the creepiest thing he has ever seen.

"What do you want?" says Benedetto, wondering how the hell he got tied up. "What the fuck do you want?"

The bird just stares, and says nothing. Benedetto closes his eyes, turns away. When he opens them back up, the bird is clutching a large dental drill in its beak, and he passes out.

SLIDE #14

Voices fade in and out. Brusque male voices, clipped and tough, yes; and one soft, quavering female voice, trying hard to maintain a good front but on the brink of losing it.

"This is exactly the way we found him, ma'am. I don't know what happened here. It looks, frankly, like he tied *himself* up, which is a neat little trick to pull off. It's like he wanted to die here and make it look like someone else was responsible."

"I don't understand why he would do such a thing." Sobs.

"Frankly, neither do we. But he appears to be alive, and when he comes to, you can ask him yourself."

"So you're leaving him here?"

"No ma'am. He's already escaped from prison once. He's going to maximum security, most likely. I'd say your goodbyes, too, because odds are they'll fry him before you can say Jack Robinson."

"Oh my God!"

"Your name, ma'am?"

"Carol Ann Beckenberger."

"How do you know this man?"

"He was a friend."

"How *good* a friend?" Salaciously.

"That's my business!" Snapping.

"Watch your tone, sister."

"What are you doing with him?"

"What do you think? He's going with us. He's going in the paddy wagon. Straight to Folsom. Maximum security, like I said. You don't listen all that good." Then the grunts, gasps, and swearing of two men trying to put a man into a stretcher and lift him—a man who, though more compact than either of them, is somehow heavier than both.

SLIDE #15

Carol is the star witness in the trial to determine whether Benedetto gets the chair. The DA, a slick individual in a sharkskin suit, too much hair oil, and a pencil mustache, cross-examines her as Benedetto watches. She's in tears. She's talking to Benedetto as much as anyone, though she doesn't let on. She's wearing a, for her, shockingly conservative outfit consisting of a black cover-up dress, black gloves, and a black veil, looking for all the world like she's already a widow.

"Tell the court," the DA leers, "about your relationship with the defendant."

"I was in love with him... We were going to be married."

"He told you that?"

"Yes, he promised me and I have no doubt it was true." Tears and bawling.

"Did you have a ...physical relationship with the defendant?"

"I've never denied that. I was lonely. We both were."

"And in that time, did he ever hurt you physically? Did he ever slap, kick, beat, punch, harm you in any way?"

"No, he did not."

"Thank carefully, please. Justice rests on your answer."

Carol's eyes rolled back in her head. "No. Nothing that I can think of. He's a sweetheart. He's an angel."

"And yet this same angel that you speak of has murdered not one but two men, all while claiming that a bird told him to do so, not just any bird but a bird with secret information about the future of the human race! Is he, then, claiming nothing less than a revelation? Is he a sort of self-styled *prophet*, embarking on the launch of a new *religion*?" He used the words contemptuously. "If that's what's happening here, perhaps I can understand why individuals had to die for reasons inexplicable to the rest of us. After all, every religion needs a martyr."

Carol had now stopped sobbing. On her face in the place of grief was a hard look. Suddenly, she'd had enough. She'd been around the block enough times to recognize when she was being had.

"You think you've got all of us wrapped around your little finger, don't you?" she said. "You think you're so smart with your goddam fancy law degree and your goddam fancy suit. But you don't have a thing on us, not a thing. Our relationship is innocent and pure, and if he's a little mixed up, so what? He was following his heart."

"Your honor, I respectfully object that the witness is out of order," said the lawyer smugly.

"Objection overruled," said the judge, a rail-thin, bespectacled, overworked-looking individual who probably should have retired 10 years ago.

"Thank you, your honor," Carol continued, her hard look getting harder by the minute. "I know my Bennie killed a man, two men. And I know he may look like a crazy person for other reasons besides. Hell, he does to me. But that don't change the fact that he ain't said those things to hurt people. He said them because he believes in something, however goofy. How many of you people can say the same thing? Sure you believe in Jesus and go to church, because no one thinks it's ridiculous that he was born without a father, or that he died and then came back to life three days later. Or you believe in Moses who parted the Red Sea and his god that made one candle last for eight nights. So, why not a giant bird?" she asked with a pronounced Yiddish lilt.

"That's enough," said the judge. "The witness may stand down."

"I rest my case," the lawyer said, loudly, showily, and gratuitously. He dusted off his hands and sat down, the sleeves of his shiny suit practically squeaking as they rubbed against its front panels.

SLIDE #16

One of Benedetto's most vibrant, and virulent, memories keeps on surfacing like a bad dream. In fact, he's relived it so many times he's uncertain whether it *is* a dream.

He's in basic training, right after having been inducted into This Man's Navy. He's learning how to shoot a turret gun in order to kill as many of the enemy as possible. To that end, there are 10 targets. The targets look like the individuals he's, symbolically, meant to be taking down: a raging red-faced Hitler, an apoplectic Mussolini with spaghetti sauce staining his shirt (Benedetto takes a little offense at this, as a true-blue Italian American); and Tojo, the most stridently racist caricature of them all, with slanted eyes and buck teeth, a poster boy for xenophobia if there ever was one.

"Ready, aim, fire!" barked the drill sergeant over and over again, as he and the rest of his platoon emptied their machine guns into the passive cardboard targets. Benedetto shot them in the face, through the heart, in the guts, with a frown of bloodthirsty rage on his face as the sergeant had taught him. "Yaaaaaaaaaa," he screamed—a primal wail that drowned out the ship's motor and indeed the screams of his fellow sailors and the noise of their own turret guns and just about everything else.

Then Benedetto came to the last target, the only one he hadn't filled with holes yet. It was a little boy, a little Japanese orphan. Benedetto knew exactly why it was there: to wipe out any last shred of compassion, compassion a soldier couldn't afford to have because by the time he'd fought that battle within himself, he'd be dead. It should have been easy to shoot because Benedetto knew it was just a piece of cardboard, but he just couldn't bring himself to do it. He stood there, aiming, looking around, trying to buy time while his fellow sailors eyed him suspiciously.

"What's the matter, Benedetto?" the drill sergeant scoffed. "You do want to be a sailor in This Man's Navy, don't you? Because it's a little late to get out now."

"Yes sir."

"You're not developing unhealthy sympathies for the enemy just because you've got some Eye-talian blood in you, are you?"

"No sir."

"Well then, you ought to be able to shoot that little Jap orphan full o' holes, boy. Now do what I tell you before I send you to KP, and that's if you're lucky because I'll have every right to court-martial you and if you put me in a bad mood I just might!"

Benedetto had no inclination whatsoever to shoot the orphan, whereas he had every inclination in the world to shoot the drill sergeant. But he resisted doing so because he knew it would not only mean a court-martial but most likely the electric chair. The military didn't mess around with that sort of situation and they definitely didn't tolerate insubordination from a new recruit.

Benedetto did what he had to do, as he attracted more and more attention. His face was hot with shame, compounded by years of mass and confession and Catholic school. He would be a good sailor and kill the way Our Lord Jesus would, if He were ever to join the Navy.

Benedetto took aim, yelled a Tarzan-like battle cry as loud as he could muster, then squeezed his trigger with a slow, sure hand. The result was deafening. For some reason, it seemed even louder than usual, even though it was the same turret gun he'd always been using and so had everyone else. It was like a thunderstorm heard through a pair of amplified electric earphones, combined with the sound of ten thousand steel balls falling on a sheet of glass.

Benedetto looked at what he had done. The cardboard was so full of bullets you couldn't recognize what it was supposed to represent anymore. Not one had missed. Benedetto should have been pleased.

He was not pleased. He broke down and cried. Then he cried some more.

Then he threw up.

"Oh, for Pete's sake," said the drill sergeant. "Class frigging dismissed."

SLIDE #17

Benedetto had been just a wee chico of two when his grandma had given him a bath toy, a washing mitt in the shape of a yellow canary. She had knitted it herself, and she had looked so proud when she'd given it to him on Christmas morning, right after he'd gorged himself on American candy: those striped crunchy balls that spit out a sweet gooey gel when you bit into them, candy canes and peppermint disks, Chunkies, Clark bars whose ingredients listed the vaguely adult and evil-sounding "chocolate liquor," sugary gum in 17 tooth-rotting flavors. Then there were the oranges and tangerines that she'd had in Sicily but never thought she'd see again, juicier and sweeter than the smaller, sour oranges she remembered from home. Just like Americans to do everything up bigger and better, even something as unimportant as an orange. But while it was the sweets and oranges that caught Benedetto's fancy (in that order), the canary bath glove was what stood the test of time. The snacks were gone by Christmas dinner, but the canary lasted well into next Christmas, and the Christmas after that and the one after that, until it faded and became threadbare and ultimately got tossed into the ragbag Benedetto's grandmother kept.

And why did Benedetto keep the little canary washcloth so long? Because it reminded him of *life*. Because it made him feel *alive.* Because he would spend ten, twenty, thirty minutes, even an hour, washing certain parts of his body, parts that Father Bonaduce told him he should not even *touch* much less wash, sinful parts, bad parts, parts that the nuns at school would pull his hair out and slap his hand with their steel rulers for daring to touch. But these parts didn't feel bad. They felt good, very good, and after all he wasn't actually touching himself, was he? The canary was touching him. The canary was not him, it was Other, it was an Entity unto itself, but he couldn't just keep fooling himself that way, no, in order for the ruse to work and for him to pull one over on his own conscience, the Canary had to really come to life, with a voice, and a mind, and thoughts and feelings and ideas and (Father Bonaduce would really belt him one if he told him this) a *soul...*

SLIDE #18

The desk was covered with books, papers, and photographs. Many of the documents were covered with the vestiges of various rubber stamps: "Approved," "Denied," "Pending," "Released," "Transferred." An enormous ashtray sat near one edge of the desk and both Laramie and Grady used it to ash the five-cent cigars they smoked as they worked. Both were in shirtsleeves with plenty of blue steel stubble and sweating like hogs, Laramie tall and malnourished, Grady short, stumpy and rounded. Laramie wore suspenders over his yellowing shirt, giving him the air of a forlorn clown.

"Storniolo—denied. Vincent—denied. Beck—transferred to Folsom, he's a bad apple of the lowest order. Same thing with Sewell. The two of them ought to be very cozy sharing a cell together." Grady stamped his ink pad, then a document, then his ink pad again, keeping up as best he could.

Eventually Grady looked up. "Don't we ever release *anyone*?"

"Not on my watch. They're in here for a reason." Laramie lit up a new stogie with the butt of the old one.

"Then why the Jesus do we have the "Released" stamp in the first place?"

"Got me, pal. All those stamps were made a long time ago. Things have changed. People have gone to the birds. This ain't the good old days anymore."

"You can say that again." Grady paused as he held up a document he hadn't seen before. "What about this one? Benedetto...what's his story? Anything there worth writing home about?"

"Oh, you mean the crazy one," Laramie said. "Ain't you heard about him? He's the one says a giant bird talks to him. It ain't no kind of scam, neither. He thinks it's real. A giant bird that tells him the future. Kinda adds a new meaning to *crazy as a loon*, don't it?" Laramie guffaws at his own gag.

"It do, at that," Grady replies. "What's this bird tell him? That the future's all sunshine and roses? Does he get to be president and win the Nobel Prize and the Miss America too?"

"Naw," Laramie says. "He don't win nothing. He loses and so does everybody else. Doom and gloom as far as the eye can see. So says the bird."

"Maybe he oughta try one a' those new shock treatments, what they call electro, convulsive, therapy," said Grady, pronouncing each syllable like a separate word, real scientific-like. "That'll fix him up good."

"That's a bright idea," Laramie concurs. "It might be the first bright idea you ever came up with."

"Thanks for nothin'."

"Give him the mental. That'll send him on his way."

And Laramie finds the "PSYCHO" stamp and stamps Benedetto's sheet good and hard. It leaves a nice big red mark. He stamps it a couple of more times for good measure, until it looks like it has the measles.

"There we go," he said. "That ought to fry that bird in his brain. By the time they're done with him, it'll be ready for mashed potatoes and gravy."

And the two of them proudly pause for a moment to admire their handiwork.

SLIDE #19

Benedetto has managed to slide under the radar for a long time. But today, a couple of nameless thugs show up at his new cell in the Psych Ward, where he only just got transferred a couple of days ago. The cell is outfitted even worse than average, with no razor since you could slit your wrist with it and no sink since you could split your head open. The most they'll give you is a toilet and even that's little better than a glorified hole in the ground. There's also no cellmate, which for Benedetto is mostly a good thing, since he's a loner by nature. He's had lots of time to sit here and contemplate his crimes against society, of which he believes there are none since clearly the shrink deserved to die, and in a much more horrible way than Benedetto killed him; but in spite of his clear innocence, people all around him keep on insisting that he's guilty. He also often thinks of Carol, her beautiful body straight from the Italian version of heaven, the Renaissance one, her kind ways and easy-going demeanor, her always sparkling and entertaining conversation. Will he ever see her again? It's not looking good.

As the men in white button-down uniforms and caps approach the door, Benedetto's bird appears to him straight out of the James Stewart movie *Harvey*, eight feet tall, neck butting up against the ceiling so that the head is bent down at a 45 degree angle.

"This is it, kid," tweets the bird. "I'm getting on the big bus. So long. Arrivederci, paisan'. Sayonara. Happy trails to you, until, we meet, again," singing the last part a la Gene Autry on the radio.

"Don't go."

"I can't help it. They're gonna fry your brain with electricity. It'll put you to sleep and then you won't know two plus two or your own name, let alone that you ever knew me."

"What now?"

"I suggest you get a camera. Take pictures of everything you see. They'll help you remember. Carol can probably bring you one, if you call and ask her nicely."

"But they're taking me away now."

"This is test day. They'll cut your hair, do some preliminary measurements. The Big Event is tomorrow. Give you some time to build up a little suspense."

"What about the future?"

"What about it? We can warn people, but let's face it, most won't listen. You humans aren't very bright. You're programmed to have sex, fight, stuff raw berries into your faces and maybe once in a while catch a squirrel. Asking you to do anything else, like planning more than five minutes out or making a sacrifice for the greater good, just goes in one ear and out the other. But if it helps you feel better, I'll appear to other people once in a while - not just you. It'll help if they take a *lot* of drugs. I hear some guy in Sweden invented a good one."

"I'll take that under advisement."

"Now go," says the bird. "Forget about the world. You're too sensitive for it anyway."

"Now you're just saying what you think I want to hear," Benedetto retorts.

"See what I mean?" And, with a little flap of its bright yellow wings, the bird vanishes into the fetid air of the cell.

SLIDE #20

A storm creeps in unlike any the world has seen to date, an eerie, unnerving combination of snow, rain, hurricane winds, and high tides, outing all power and turning the clock back 100 years but without the benefit of horse-drawn transportation. Carol looks to the sky, wondering where her life will go from here. Will Benedetto ever get on the straight and narrow? Better just to cut bait and move on.

But she will miss him so.

The sky fills with roiling gray clouds. Tiny drizzle drops begin to cloud her eyes. A gull calls.

SLIDE #21

Benedetto recalls his military training. That was an orderly, predictable period of his life. Perhaps the *most* orderly and predictable.

Perhaps this is why he now remembers it so fondly.

Here is what Benedetto remembers. A tent camp with a fallen tree. A take-no-bullshit yet kind-hearted sergeant that when he told you to drop and give him 20 you did it, not just because you would get court-martialed if you didn't but because you wanted to make him proud. A series of strength and endurance drills: climbing trees and crossing rivers via rope ladders, running track and obstacle courses, Thousand Mile Hikes, calisthenics from reveille until taps. In between there was briefing, debriefing, gatherings where he was honored and those where he was called on the carpet, long poker games, he lost money but had a fine time doing it, smoking too many cheap cigars and drinking too much beer from the PX.

And most of all he remembers the slide shows. He'd never seen a slide projector in civilian life, they didn't really exist yet as a tool to torture your neighbor with vacation photos, but here one was, a Kodak Carousel manufactured for the military, specially commissioned by the DOD. It was a thing of beauty, fatigue-green with a round cartridge that rotated, dropping the slides one by one into the projection chamber where they were hit by light and appeared big as life on the collapsible screen in front of Benedetto's platoon. Then they disappeared to be replaced by more slides: some identifying trumped-up enemies, some illustrating plans of attack with richly hand-drawn maps fairly blazing with cartographic skill and draftsmanship, some eye-popping title cards, some cartoons verging on pornographic with outrageous hips and breasts urging soldiers to be careful of diseases and loose lips around enemy women.

The slide projector was Benedetto's favorite memory of the military, its polite but insistent *click, click, click* representing a welcome stability he'd never seen. Not in his tempestuous and bizarre family life with his parents at each others' throats, often literally so with actual razors, his mother often winning; and certainly not after. He misses that feeling. And now it was gone, and would never come back.

SLIDE #22

On the hard white table covered with butcher paper, Benedetto feels uncomfortable. No, uncomfortable is an understatement. He feels deliberately discomfited. Someone is trying to take away his dignity, make him less than human.

"Hold still," grumbles a white-suited and white-faced attendant. "Don't wiggle so much. This is all about accuracy. You don't want it to hurt, do you?"

"I thought it was supposed to hurt."

"It isn't, not if they do it right."

"How often is that?"

"Not very." Blase.

The camera is right there in Benedetto's hands. He's requested permission to bring it along to the ECT room and no one can really think of any laws against that, as much as they would like to. Having got them on a technicality, Benedetto photographs, from a supine position, the art deco lighting fixture, the faces of the operators, his own face, and various paintings and decorative objects around the room.

"What's this all about?" asks the attendant.

"Posterity," Benedetto answers with a straight face. The attendant shrugs. Wackos. You never can tell what they'll pull next.

SLIDE #23

"Whatever they do," Benedetto says, "don't let them take my camera." But no one hears.

SLIDE #24

A passing 13-year-old boy picks up the tiny Japanese camera lying in the sand. Some tourist must have left it there. The boy has heard of these, vaguely. They're called *35, m, m.* He's not sure why or what the *m's* stand for. The camera is black and silver and smaller than any camera he's ever seen on these shores including the Kodak Brownie, small enough to fit in one hand or even a big coat pocket.

"Hey dad," he calls out. But dad is already far ahead, walking back toward the mother on her beach blanket with a handful of shells, the mother smoking and peering at her watch through movie star dark glasses.

Sighing, the kid holds the camera to his face, looks through the viewfinder, and snaps a picture of the ocean. The tide creeps in, further and further.

7 SUPPORT OUR BOYS OVERSEAS!

Dr. Williams looked down at the book he was reading. At least, he thought it was a book. He had lost his reading glasses and there wasn't a place around to get a good pair, not anymore. Schwab's and Rexall's were both fresh out, not just of reading glasses but of just about everything including two cents plain. You went in and the bareness of the walls and shelves just assaulted you. Even the trademark smell of women's face powder and cheap sugary freezer-burned ice cream was weaker than it used to be. Shortages.

What had he been reading, he wondered? Not *Moby Dick*, it wasn't big enough for that. Not *A Tale of Two Cities* either, and nothing French. He really wasn't sure, it had been so long since he'd been able to see the print.

"Honey," he called to his wife Clara in the kitchenette, "what was I reading?"

"I dunno," she said, not hostile but certainly sleepy. "A book."

That wasn't really the answer Dr. Williams was looking for, but Clara couldn't be blamed for being a little on edge. All she had had in life was her kitchen. She had loved to put up jams and jellies and pickles, make roasts and hams, concoct soups and stews, confect cookies and cakes, and try exotic European dishes she could barely pronounce. Now, thanks to the new wave of war shortages, all that was being taken away from her.

For a while, it had given them strength to keep in mind that it was all to help their boy Allen beat the Nazis. Then the news had come. Since then, the days had blended into a dark, Spam-filled rut.

"I miss cooking," Clara said.

"I miss *eating* your cooking," Dr. Williams replied. He meant it, too. Clara could cook better than pretty much anyone he'd ever met, certainly better than his mother, who'd never met a piece of meat she couldn't turn into a hunk of charcoal or a dessert she couldn't turn into a rock. Now, all their meals were variations of Spam: Spam and rice, Spam and egg noodles, Spam and grits. Spam and any dry, cookable starch that wouldn't go bad, maybe with powdered eggs. At breakfast, cold cereal and oatmeal were out since you couldn't get fresh milk or cream, and the dried stuff was disgusting. Fresh fruits and vegetables were often off the menu, though you could come by pickles if you were willing the pay the price. Dr. Williams was trying to grow a Victory Garden of cauliflower, turnips, and radishes in the backyard, with varying degrees of success. His knowledge of biology did help, but he'd grown up a city boy with no real plots of land to cultivate, and seemed to have a brown thumb that turned out only tiny roots and withered greens.

"What do you say we go for a walk?" Dr. Williams suggested to his wife. "Get our mind off our troubles?"

"Sure, OK," said Clara.

Dr. Williams and his wife had retired to a small but lovely home in rural Vermont. It was near a small but pristine woods, and the two of them took a walk there nearly every day. They enjoyed watching the colors of the leaves change in time with the seasons, and were reminded of the changes in their own lives: their high-spirited youth together in Boston, their marriage, the birth of their son, and the day he marched off to war.

And didn't come back.

They held hands, as they were wont to do, and shared a cigarette as they began their walk into the forest the same as any other walk on any other day. They did not lock their door. They didn't have to. Their hamlet was small enough that if anyone even set foot in the wrong house, everyone would know about it right away.

Now Dr. Williams and Clara were hungry when they left the house, because they were more than a little weary of eating tinned meat; and they became even hungrier as they made their way into the woods. They were beginning to wish they hadn't let their monotony lead them astray, since ultimately even boring food is better than no food at all. About a half mile or so into the woods, just as their appetites were beginning to get the better of them and they were about to turn to each other and head back, they noticed a tree bearing delicious-looking fruit. They had never seen it before, but it looked like a cross between an apple, a pear, and a fresh fig.

"You know," started Dr. Williams in an opening gambit.

"I've never seen anything," replied Clara.

"Of course, curiosity killed," Dr. Williams shot back at himself.

"He who hesitates," Clara retorted.

"The best things in life."

"That's what *I'm* saying."

The most unnerving thing about the fruit was that it was hanging there, plump and ripe looking, at the end of autumn, really the beginning of winter in fact, when all the apples and pears and other fruit were rotting on the ground. But it wasn't unnerving enough to prevent Dr. Williams from picking it and taking a little tiny bite; then, after noticing its sweet taste and total lack of resemblance to anything poisonous, a bigger and juicier bite, so juicy in fact that the liquid ran down his chin as though he were a sloppy baby.

"Why yes I will, thank you," Clara said, and she helped herself to some as well, ultimately eating even more than Dr. Williams. That was fine with him, since he thought a healthy appetite was attractive and had told Clara so many times.

After they had finished the fruit and the sucked-dry core lay on the ground covered with a thin layer of gnawed pulp, Dr. Williams and Clara belched contentedly. They hadn't expected the fruit to be so filling. They felt like they had eaten a coconut rather than an apple or pear, and the fruit had even seemed to contain some protein, so sated were they. They felt like they'd eaten a steak. So it didn't surprise them at all when they got an irresistible craving for a nap; and they were so warmly snuggled in their coats and scarves and comfy knitted woolen hats (all created from miracle man-made fibers discovered during the war) that they weren't even cold when they collapsed onto the thin layer of freshly fallen snow and went right to sleep.

"Goodnight, Doc," Clara said, using her fond nickname for him.

"Goodnight, sweetie pie," Dr. Williams replied.

And, holding hands and touching their faces to one another, they drifted off to sleep.

#

Private Allen Williams searched in his pockets for his engraved Zippo. He wasn't craving a smoke. He just wanted some warmth. It was 20 below in Amsterdam, where he was stationed, and even under his standard-issue parka he was chilled to the bone. He cupped his hand around the delicate flame and held it to his cheek, trying to soak up the warmth the way a towel soaks up water.

Just 17 (he had lied because he'd wanted to serve so badly and no one had argued with him), Allen was thin, pale, and stumpy, just this side of 4F. He was standing guard over the camp with Kazurinski, who was just as young, just as short, just as skinny and even paler than he was, with four eyes and a bad case of acne. He was also going prematurely bald. The two of them made quite a tableau, shivering in the freezing rain and trying not to lose it entirely.

"This weather is really wet and cold," Allen said.

"So's your mother," Kazurinski shot back, and Allen threw the Zippo at him mostly because it was the only item to hand.

"Smart," said Kazurinski. "It's 20 below and we need fire. If that lighter breaks, we break. You know that, doncha?"

"Yeah, I know it," Allen said. "I just don't want to believe it." He dove for the Zippo before it could sink too deeply into the snow and wiped it on his heavy wool sleeve. "Look," he said. "I signed up before they could even draft me. I came here to fight dirty Krauts who want to take away our American way of life. But where are they all? Where are all these Nazis that I'm supposed to be afraid of? All we've been doing is guarding a deserted outpost in the middle of nowhere. It's a waste of our time, our energy and our intelligence."

"Sure," Kazurinski nodded. "Military intelligence."

"That's very goddamn funny," said Allen. "I hope you'll remember it after the Nazis invade the US and turn half our cars into Volkswagens. I just want one chance to be a hero."

They stared into the silent, falling snow, their eyes and thoughts drifting. Really both should have gone to sleep hours ago. Their vision was fading and their thought processes were scattered at best. Allen looked up and saw the stars starting to spin. He was a New England country boy, used to seeing the stars, but he wasn't used to seeing them revolve around his head the way planets revolve around the sun.

Eventually Kazurinski lit up a smoke as a kind of peace offering. It flared in spite of the rain and smelled a little stale too, but he offered it to Williams, who was glad to share it.

About half an hour into their mutual silent reverie, or maybe it was an hour or possibly two, there was a noise in the bushes. At first both of them thought it was some sort of wild animal, maybe a badger or a skunk or even some kind of Kraut animal they hadn't run across in the States. But in fact they kept hearing it, and it was rhythmic and getting louder, and they looked at each other at about the same time as they realized the noise could only be human footsteps.

"Nobody ever comes around here," Allen whispered.

"Well, they must," said Kazurinski with typical bravado. "Why the shit would they have had us stake this place out?"

"There's no soldiers to capture or kill, nothing to steal, no buildings to take. Just a couple of bum privates standing guard where no one else wants to. Freezing rain not fit for man or beast, no strategic importance... No gold, no jewelry, no stores of food or tobacco..." Allen took a moment to meditate on the stub of his cigarette, then flicked it away. "I just don't know what the point would be."

The footsteps, which had temporarily stopped during the conversation, were now louder than ever. Allen and Kazurinski immediately drew themselves up to their full height. Oddly, the sound seemed to be coming from behind them, where before it had been at around 1:00. They each marked the other's reaction, then removed the safeties from their rifles.

"Must be a sneaky frigging Kraut," Kazurinski said.

"They're getting sneakier every day," Allen agreed.

The footsteps got loud enough to be a few feet away. The two looked down their sights at the unlockable, unsecured door to the abandoned genever warehouse where they were hiding. They saw a flash of pale, untoned, almost pearly flesh and, without thinking about it and exactly as they had been trained to do, fired.

The victim, who had been holding the doorknob at the time, collapsed to the floor with an audible thump. Allen and Kazurinski quietly approached the resulting corpse, keeping their rifles aimed right at it just in case it wasn't quite as dead as they thought.

Both of them bumped the corpse in the stomach with the butts of their rifles, looking for reflexes, and it stayed motionless. There was only one problem.

The dead thing lying there in front of them had been an 11-year-old girl.

"Oh my God," said Allen.

"Jesus Christ," said Kazurinski.

"We just murdered a kid," he said. "Not even a teenager."

"Godammit," Kazurinski commiserated.

"Sugar and spice, and all that stuff."

"Yep. Did you feel her pulse?"

Allen felt for a pulse. There was none. She was a lump. He stood up and removed his helmet for a moment of silence. Kazurinski instinctively crossed himself and said the Lord's prayer.

They looked at each other. Shaking, Allen fumbled for his walkie talkie.

"What are you doing?" Kazurinski immediately barked.

"I'm going to radio it in," Allen said. "I know we can't save her, but we can at least let the chaplain know she's dead and have her given a decent burial. We don't know what to do with her." He looked down at the girl's dark, indistinctly European features. "Hell, she might even be a Jewess."

"I doubt that, and even if she is, what's that got to do with the price of tea in China? We're not calling this in. No one knows who the hell she is. Look at the dirt, look at the filth, look at how scuffed up she is." He kicked at the girl's torn, ragged frock. "No one's gonna miss her. No parents, no guardians, no relatives, probably no friends. Leave it be."

"What are we going to do with her body, then?" Allen asked incredulously, knowing full well that he was ceding authority, by implication, to this barely-a-man - this teenage boy, really - who was no less callow than he and a damn sight more callous on top of it.

"You leave that to me."

Allen, whose gaze had been on the splatter of organs and flesh in front of them both, looked up to meet Kazurinski's gaze. What he saw was the steely determination he had seen on the battlefield many times, but also something that frightened him: a cool, calculating lust, slicked over with a superficial nonchalance as transparent was it was phony.

"Maybe I will and maybe I won't," Allen said.

"Just what the hell's that supposed to mean?"

"It's supposed to mean you'll do as you're told."

"Who says? We're both privates."

"Not anymore." Kazurinski produced an insignia from his pocket and displayed it proudly. "I haven't had a chance to sew it on yet. I'm a sergeant now. Got promoted last Tuesday."

"Promoted? What for?"

"That's my business," Kazurinski replied tightly. "Let me suggest you tend to your own, which involves going outside, standing guard, and performing night watch duties. I suggest you don't come back in here until you're finished, which will be at 0900 hours. Is that clear, private?"

Already shaken up by the murder itself, Allen now found himself absolutely paralyzed. The words were like frozen metal blocks caught in his throat and he couldn't cough them out.

"I said, is that clear?"

Allen's "Yes, sir" was the most half-hearted response he had given to any command, ever, during the whole of his military history. Head hung, his rifle haphazardly swinging, he began to shuffle out of the room. It's inhuman, he reasoned to himself. The man is a monster. He's desecrating this girl's memory. And yet, that's all it is, really. A memory, no more, no less. He may be a necrophile and a pedophile, but thank God she's not alive to feel the pain, to witness the violence.

Allen was just about to open the heavy, rusted warehouse door and let himself out when Kazurinski addressed him. "And private," he said, "don't even think about barging in. If you have to use the latrine, you can go outside in the snow. I'll see you at 0900 hours. Is that crystal clear?"

That about did it. Allen's hands shook and his whole field of vision contracted to a fuzzy, fist-size oval as his limbs tensed up and his heart raced. Adrenalin, he thought, as though outside his own body analyzing its processes. The fight-or-flight response. They taught us all about it in basic training, but I thought maybe I'd have to use the knowledge in the field, fighting Krauts or wild animals. I never thought it would come up with a fellow U.S. soldier.

Allen turned to face Kazurinski, lifted his rifle, looked through the sight, locked, and loaded.

Kazurinski had clearly been prepared for the eventuality. "Put the rifle down," he said. "Be a good soldier. Think about it, Williams. What are you getting out of this? You'll be court-martialed, and for what? The girl is already dead. Put the rifle down now."

This Allen did not do. Instead he counted to three—quickly, lest he lose his advantage against Kazurinski, whom he knew from basic training was an accomplished master at hand-to-hand and even hand-to-weapon fighting—and then fired. He fired and reloaded and fired and reloaded. He fired directly into Karuzinski's head until almost all of his ammo was gone and then, because it constituted poetic justice, into his genitals as well.

"Congratulations on your promotion, Sergeant Kazurinski," he said.

There were now *two* puddles of leaking blood and gooey organs on the floor. Even in the cold, the smell was beginning to get to Allen. He pushed the warehouse door open and propped it there with a big rock. Cold air rushed in, causing him to see the fog of his breath. He had thought he was cold inside the warehouse, but now he realized that his and Kazurinski's body heat and breath had been warming it for days without his even having relished it. The air from outside was excruciatingly painful. It felt like it was going to burn his face off the way frozen nitrogen gas might, yet he needed the fresh air and almost stopped feeling nauseated when it rushed into the room.

Allen looked around. He had committed two murders, there was no denying it. He had grown up a pacifist, trained never to raise a hand in anger no matter what the cause. His father, Dr. Williams, who worked at the local hospital, had seen far too much carnage and destruction in what he always just called "the War" or "the Great War." It always made him sick just to talk about, his eyes welling up with what he referred to as "loose tear ducts." Then there was his mother, a model of compassion, who had taught him never to hurt a living thing, not even an ant or a spider, because all of them were cut from the same cloth and besides, who knew but that the Hindus in India were right and you might be reincarnated as one yourself someday. She was the gentlest person Allen had ever known, always following her own creed, never spanking her children or using corporal punishment of any kind, even during trying times when other women might easily have been tempted to. Allen had worshipped her and had himself never hit a person in anger, even when bullied or brutalized in grade school, middle school high school, and the army. As a matter of fact, it occurred to him, there wasn't a year or phase of his life when he hadn't been kicked, pushed, or shoved around by someone, beaten or browbeaten, bashed or smashed. Now, after being pushed down for twenty years, all his worst impulses had finally come to a head. He had slaughtered an innocent little girl as well as a fellow army buddy who, though an insane, violent and sexually demented pervert, had at least the right to a fair trial.

"This is where I get off," Allen thought. He'd had 21 years where he'd tried to live a decent and upstanding life and now it had all been shot to hell. In fact, he mentally corrected himself, he'd shot it all to hell himself with his own rifle. What chance would he have now? By the time he got out of prison even with time off for good behavior, his life would be more than half over to say nothing of the ensuing court-martial. He wished to hell he'd died as a war hero, but that hadn't been in the cards.

Allen locked and loaded the rifle and turned it on himself, pointing it into the underside of his chin. It was nasty, freezing and metallic and unyielding. He could smell the almost electric tang of the gunmetal and the evil richness of the oil. He looked around. The room was suddenly smaller, the walls closer to Allen's head with no other soldier to pace back and forth marking the space. Blood was rapidly spreading to cover the entire floor filling the room with an even stronger iron stink, and Allen was sure he was going to add the contents of his stomach to the mess any minute.

This is *your* responsibility, he thought. You caused this.

You're no better than Mussolini or Tojo.

You're no better than Hitler.

With that, Allen pulled the trigger. The last thing he saw, right before he died, was the eleven-year-old girl's beautiful face, pale and slightly sickly, covered with red chocolate smears and splatters, her hair caked with dirt and grease. He had saved her body from the worst indignity a person could ever suffer, he thought.

He would not die in vain.

#

Dr. Williams and Clara awoke at just about the same time. Their bellies felt full of apple-pear pulp and their heads felt full of cotton and sawdust.

Dr. Williams opened his eyes and saw that the sky was a perfect blue without even a wisp of cloud and felt that the air was agreeably cool with just a touch of breeze. He looked over at his wife, who seemed to be equally enraptured. Her hair was a rat's nest from her having tossed and turned on the ground all night, and what little makeup she wore was running and smeared, but otherwise she looked all right.

"We must have slept all night," said Dr. Williams, trying to keep the conversation normal. His heart was pumping like crazy and he could feel it inside his rib cage. His eyes were watering and tearing as though they didn't belong to him anymore.

"I think we did," Clara replied.

"Must have been the fruit."

"Must have been."

"I had some strange dreams."

"That's funny," Clara said. "Me too."

They paused to take each other in. "You first," Dr. Williams said.

"I dreamed about Allen in the war."

"What about Allen?" Dr. Williams asked accusingly, knowing full well what it was but not wanting to hear it confirmed.

"Well... you know how the telegram came saying that he had been a hero but that his body was too... mutilated to bring back for a proper funeral?"

"Sure."

"Well, I dreamed that's not what happened. I dreamed that Allen wasn't such a hero, wasn't such a good boy as we've thought he was."

"Go on."

"I dreamed that he....ohhh!" Suddenly Clara broke down crying into Dr. Williams's arms. He held her close and comforted her, her breasts suddenly feeling much smaller and drier than usual as though she had aged fifteen years overnight. "I dreamed that he killed a person. Two people. Not Germans or Japanese either," she added, too refined to use the coarse derogatory slang terms. "Regular people. An American soldier, a buddy in the same platoon, and a little...a little girl." She could barely get the word out before she simply lost all control, crying and shaking and screeching as though possessed. "A little girl, John." She buried her face in his already dew-damp shirt and soaked it in her tears.

"I'm sorry, dear," Dr. Williams consoled her. "That sounds terrible. Just frightful. I'm glad you're all right."

"What about you?" Clara said through her sobs. "You said you had a dream, too."

"I don't really remember," Dr. Williams lied. "It's all a bit of a blur. I think maybe Allen might have been in mine, too," he added, always tucking the flavor of truth into a lie when he could, the way Clara tucked just a little meat into her pot pies. He was mostly a scrupulously honest man, but saving his wife's feelings was one place where he would compromise that honesty if needed.

They stood up together, Dr. Williams taking his wife's hand and helping her up. They each brushed off the front of their own clothing, and then took turns helping the other one brush the leaves, dirt, and grass off his or her back. After all, what was marriage for, he thought, if you weren't willing to groom your mate the way our primate cousins have for millions of years?

"Do you think it's true, John?" Clara asked plaintively, her eyes welling up just short of dripping a tear. "Allen's posthumous medal, the Army's telegram, was it all a sham? Did our boy really kill a fellow American soldier and a defenseless little girl on top of it?"

"I... I don't know."

Clara stared at him. "You had the same dream, didn't you?" Her face fell apart into about five hundred million pieces. "You saw Allen pick up his rifle and shoot that American soldier, one of our own troops, in cold blood, and a little girl too. *Didn't you?*" she screamed at the top of her lungs, becoming completely unhinged for really the first time ever since Dr. Williams had known her. She sobbed and pounded her husband's chest, letting out heart-rending yowls.

"I don't know what you're talking about, darling," Dr. Williams lied. "I had a vague dream about Allen being in the army doing... army things. Nothing like what you're talking about, certainly."

"I don't believe you," Clara moaned. "What's done is done. Our only son is now not only dead but disgraced, a double murderer and of a child yet."

"Even if that were true," Dr. Williams replied, trying to keep a cool, shiny lid on top of the boiling pot of his soul, "there may be a lot we don't know. Not everything is black and white."

"Yes it is!" Clara shouted. "What are we fighting for, if not a black and white world! The Allies are good, the Axis is bad! Christians are good, the godless are bad! People of breeding and distinction are good, the, the, the lazy and shiftless are bad," she added, trying not to sound too horrible even to herself. "Is our son good or evil? Is he a horrible monster or a medal-earning hero? He cannot be both! I don't want to live in a world where he can be both!" she wailed, literally gnashing her dentures in agony.

"I love you very much, Clara," said Dr. Williams. "The sun has risen today. It's going to rise again tomorrow. And now you and I are going to go back to our lovely warm house, and our lovely life and our lovely friends. And we're going to have a good, stiff drink, and then we're never going to talk about this with anyone, ever again."

Clara looked up at him with infinitely sad, pleading eyes.

"Are we?"

She shook her head.

"Nothing happened here last night," Dr. Williams said. "Say it," he snapped.

"Nothing happened here last night," Clara repeated glumly.

"What happened here last night?"

"Nothing."

"What did we dream about last night?" he demanded.

"Nothing."

"Good girl."

And she took his hand, and together, slowly, they made their way home, pretending with all their might that their world was still the same.

8 THE UNDISPUTED TRUE LOVE CHAMPION

The lunch rush at Mack's Diner was Steve and Ruby. Every lunchtime it was the two of them and, usually, no one else. In fact, would-be customers would sometimes come in hungry for a hamburger, see Steve and Ruby chatting, and quietly slip back out, assuming they were lovers. So intimate was the appearance they presented, a stranger could hardly infer anything else. To further convince any doubters, her perfume and his bay rum after-shave lotion mixed in the air with the juices from the freshly grilled hamburgers, and anyone would have said with just a cursory sniff that the result smelled like a well-used bedroom.

The truth was that the two had known each other from grade school. In spite of Steve's being a red-blooded all-American boy and Ruby's being a relentlessly feminine girl's girl, there was nothing between them. As far as both were concerned, this was a good thing, since Ruby could complain to Steve about her man troubles and Steve could do the same with Ruby when it came to his not-always-smooth dealings with women. At 30, neither had found anyone steady to be with, which meant most who knew Ruby considered her to be more or less an old maid. While Steve could get away with fielding remarks about his canny field-playing bachelorhood, he knew that in only a few years he would be exposed as no less a bluffer than an 11-year-old boy claiming to have got under a girl's brassiere.

This particular day found Ruby and Steve picking at cheeseburgers with grilled onions and sipping cherry Cokes as they solved the world's and each other's problems. Ruby's hair was neatly set off by an emerald green dress and hat. By contrast, with Steve's necktie loose, his top button unbuttoned, and his jacket draped over one arm, he was a sloppy beatnik begging to get fired.

Mack, the cafe owner, and his wife Dora had a kind of reverse deal whereby she worked the short order grill, making burgers and tuna melts, and he took the customers' orders. He was a good schmoozer with something to say on every subject and a fairly agreeable listener as well, swapping stories like a kid around a campfire, whereas Dora was a little more taciturn and liable as not to say three whole words in an hour.

"So, young lovers," Mack said, ignoring Ruby and Steve's never so much as holding hands in his diner, "there's a contest I think you ought to enter."

"What's that?" Ruby asked drolly. "The greasy cheeseburger sour stomach competition?"

"Since you've apparently been sleeping under a rock," Mack added in a hearty, avuncular tone, "here it is." He held up today's edition of the paper, the want ads section stained with multiple coffee rings. A quarter-page display ad read:

LOVERS CONTEST!!!!
Be the World's Greatest Lovers and Win the Grand Prize
Open to all lovers, any age
Dance Competition
True Love Competition
Sign Up Today!!!!!!!!!!!!!!

"That's ridiculous," Ruby said. "I understand a dance contest, but true love? How would you determine the winner? That one doesn't even make any sense."

"I can't argue with you there," Mack said, "but there is a grand prize involved. How about it, you two?"

"We're not—" Steve began, but Ruby kicked him under the dining counter and interrupted him.

"What's the grand prize?"

"It says here, five thousand smackeroos."

"Five thousand dollars?"

"I said smackeroos," Mack said jovially, lighting a cigar. "*You* said dollars."

"That's a lot of cash," Ruby pondered. "I could vacation in Tahiti like Gaugin." (She fancied herself a painter.) "I could take off for a whole year and go native. No job, no office, just a beach full of healthy South Sea Island boys."

"We would have to split the prize two ways, of course," said Steve, who worked as a lawyer. "And naturally there'll be a small fee for *doing* the splitting, and the legal paperwork involved."

"Like fun there will," Ruby glowered.

"Anyway we're splitting the prize 50/50, or no deal," Steve said.

"Fine," Ruby said like someone stomping away from a spat.

"What dances do you know?"

"I know the rhumba, I know the samba, I know the cha-cha-cha. I'm terrible at all of them, but for $2500 I can brush up."

"Now you're talking, you lovebirds," Mack said. "I'll be honest, I don't really know who's putting this contest on or if you have a snowball's chance in H.E. double hockey sticks. Heck, I don't even know what the True Love competition involves."

"Not what it sounds like, I hope." Ruby absently rubbed the stub of her cheeseburger in a little puddle of ketchup.

"Nothing dirty or I wouldn't have mentioned it. I run a clean joint." Mac looked down at their empty plates and paid tab. "Now get outta here before I throw ya out."

"Gladly," Ruby replied playfully.

"Yeah, ya jerk," Steve echoed, but he made a big point of smiling when he said it. At 6'1", he was unusually imposing and to the casual observer was at least as wide as he was tall. How he had never become a professional linebacker was anyone's guess, but over time he'd learned that anything he said came off as quite imposing, so he was extra-careful not to appear angry or say anything mean. People who knew him casually said he was a gentle giant, but those who knew him well, like Ruby, understood his secret dry sense of humor.

"You owe me for half of that lunch," Ruby said as they left together.

"Yeah, well, when I have $2500 in my pocket I'll be glad to pay for that and every other lunch this year," Steve replied. Ruby was headed for the park, meaning she was probably going to play hooky from work, and he figured he might just as well follow suit.

"We can have free money for a year," Ruby said, with what Steve had come to know as her scheming business voice running a mile a minute. It usually appeared when she was drunk. "All we have to do is practice three hours a day for the next thirty days. We do that and we're a shoo-in to win the dance contest. As far as the true love part, Lord knows what that involves but I have no doubt we can ace that too. But no touching me, that's absolutely out, get it?"

"Don't worry, sister, you're the last woman on earth and how much bourbon did your pour in your coffee exactly?"

"Exactly all of it and the feeling's mutual. Now, let's split up the responsibilities." She talked around an unlit cigarette as she whipped a pocket notepad and pencil out of her purse. "I'll go down to that filthy little record place in the village and buy a bunch of cheap knockoff Latin dance platters. You do a little research on what this true romance part of the contest is all about. Then we'll meet back at my place and compare notes."

"Done and done."

"Bye, lover," Ruby said with the most obvious sarcasm possible.

"Bye, lover," Steve responded. And he headed back to the subway and his tiny cold-water walk-up in Hell's Kitchen.

#

Well, that's how it began, anyway. Steve went back to his apartment, made some cold flat egg noodles with cut-up pieces of salami from the corner deli, and unleashed a flood of phone calls trying to figure out who was in charge of the contest and what it was all about, particularly whether it involved kissing, which he knew was off the menu for Ruby. For Steve's part he felt that smooching Ruby would probably be like kissing his sister, and though there might be a certain illicit thrill in that, it wasn't for him. Fortunately, this was about money, not love, and the sooner he could fake the love, the sooner he would get his hands on the money.

Steve dialed the ad's number as he stomped out a cockroach trying to get its mandibles on a stray piece of salami.

"Hello," came a muffled voice. Actually, Steve's phone was so old every voice that came out of it was muffled. But this voice was particularly so, as though the other party were chewing gum, or gnawing a sandwich, or smoking a cigar, or possibly all three at once.

"Hello," Steve said. He couldn't really figure out a polite way to phrase what he wanted to ask, so there was an awkward silence on the line. Steve was almost afraid the other party would hang up on him.

"What can I do for you?" the voice grouched.

"I saw your ad in the newspaper," Steve said. "You know, for the World's Greatest Lover's Contest.

"Oh, *that,*" said the other party, as though the ad represented a tiny, unimportant, superficial part of his job and Steve should know better than to bother him with such annoying trivialities. "What about it?"

"Well, listen," Steve said. "You placed the ad with this number, and me and my..." He paused a moment, the word he wanted to use was so unnatural in relation to Ruby. "... sweetheart want to enter the contest."

"Sorry," said the voice, which seemed to have taken another giant bite of sandwich. "Contest is over." It was a very final-sounding pronouncement.

"But that doesn't make any sense," Steve complained. "According to this, the contest doesn't even *start* until two weeks from today."

"What paper you looking at?"

"What difference does it make!" Steve snapped, now convinced that the other party was trying to put something over on him. He wasn't sure about the scam or this man's angle, but clearly it couldn't be on the up-and-up or he wouldn't be advertising for an event that had already happened.

"Hang on just a moment," the voice said grudgingly. "Maybe I can sneak you in."

"Sneak us in? You just said it was over! Make up your mind."

"Listen, pal," the voice erupted. "I've got Guido up my ass about the ponies and 17 respectable business people who expect to get their cut. I'm seriously thinking about hopping on a jet to Rio so if you and your *girlfriend* want to enter my contest you'd best shut your mouth and behave yourself."

"I don't appreciate your tone," Steve replied, suddenly cowed.

"Well, I don't appreciate yours, fella. Do you want to win the money or not?"

"*Yes,*" Steve said, swallowing his pride. It took all his discipline and self-control not to hang up on this individual, clearly an unsavory element if not an out-and-out criminal. He could only imagine what Ruby would say about this. She'd probably slap his face twice, once when she heard about it and again when she actually spoke to the man or, God forbid, met him face to face.

"Well, it's no skin off my nose either way," said the voice. "Okay, here's where you show up." He named an address that sounded more like an apartment house than a business, and a time about two weeks away. He also warned Steve that absolutely no weapons of any kind would be tolerated, and then immediately appended the phrase "Wink, wink."

"Then there is the matter of our entry fee," said the voice, in a suddenly officious and businesslike tone.

"The ad didn't say anything about a fee," Steve cried. "Let me speak to the man in charge."

"*I* am the man in charge," the voice said, adding disturbingly, "if I *am* a man that is."

"All right," Steve said. "How much is the 'entry fee'?"

"50 bucks a person."

"That's highway robbery."

"That's *my* business. Are you in or out?" the voice replied.

"Fine," Steve relented. "I'm in."

"You can remit at the door," the voice said, and hung up.

That was that. Steve called the nearest Arthur Murray's and booked some dance lessons. He and Ruby were going to need them.

#

Ruby met Steve at the Arthur Murray's after work on Friday. "Thanks for keeping our little date," he said.

"This is in no way a date and you know it," Ruby said. "Don't even use that word."

"Fine, thanks for keeping our appointment then. How are you?" he asked, all ready to pour out his horror story about the ridiculous contest manager.

Ruby blushed and her eyes welled up. She fished a cigarette out of purse and lit it with a sureness that revealed a particular amount of recent practice. "I was fired today," she said. "And I have no f.u. money saved up." She smoked it down to the filter in one drag.

"I'm sorry," said Steve. "That stinks," he added emptily. He looked around, but it was still just the two of them alone in the enormous ballroom. Steve had sprung for the dance studio's expensive one-on-one tutoring to help speed them along to contest success, but the tutor himself hadn't shown up yet. "What are you going to do?"

"What am I going to do?" she echoed glumly. "I'm going to win this contest. We are. We have to. Otherwise I'm out on the street." Her face had steel in it.

"I'm game," said Steve. He had been in Ruby's apartment once or twice and it hadn't been that great to begin with. The bugs were clearly in control, there was no furniture except for a few unpacked cardboard boxes and stacks of books, and the water from the pipes ran orange.

"I can't dance to save my life, but you told me you could, so we have a good shot."

"I lied," Ruby said.

"You lied? Why?! So you don't have any dance experience and neither do I? We might as well just walk in the contest door with big "*Loser*" signs plastered all over us. How are we going to convince the world we're even a couple if we can't even dance together? That's the lowest bar there is and everyone knows it. We're done," Steve appended. "We're not doing it. How can you even enter a dance contest, much less win it?"

"I've done better," Ruby countered. "I've entered a unicycle race and won. Do you think I'd ever ridden a unicycle before? I entered a novel writing contest and had my work published nationally, in addition to a nice stipend. It was the first thing I'd ever written unless you count some long letters. I even won a log rolling contest once, beating out some lumberjacks, male ones."

"How did you manage that?" Steve said, more than a little impressed by the thought of her tiny, scrawny, untoned frame pulling this off.

"Will power," she said.

The dance tutor arrived at the ballroom. He was about 6 feet 5 inches with an impeccable, tailored sharkskin suit and a pencil mustache. Steve couldn't decide whether the man's last job had been as a floorwalker at Macy's or a used car dealer. "Well hello, this must be the happy couple," he gushed, sounding for all the world like The Great Gildersleeve. "I suppose you want to learn to dance for your upcoming wedding reception. Well, well, well! When's the big day?"

"When hell freezes over," Ruby exclaimed, staring daggers at him.

"You've got yourself a live one there," Gildersleeve said, cupping a hand to Steve's ear. "Confidentially, I wouldn't be surprised if she were a regular *hellcat* in the sack. *HAY-ull, CAT*," he added for emphasis, giving the word at least three syllables. He broke away from Steve to address them as a couple. "Now, friends, why don't you show me what you know. What can you do at least a little of? That's a good place to begin. The waltz? The foxtrot?"

"The Lindy Hop," Ruby bragged.

"The Lindy Hop? Oooh, that's a tough one. And so *new.* Are you sure that's something you want to do? Not that I wouldn't *looove* to see it. I just wouldn't want you to hurt yourselves."

Steve looked at Ruby with one eyebrow practically coming off the top of his head. An inveterate and compulsive liar, she had just told him she couldn't dance a step and was now bragging to this total stranger about doing a complex dance that challenged even professionals.

"All right then, kiddos," Gildersleeve proclaimed, "let's do it to it." And he walked to the sidelines to let them take over the dance floor, setting the phonograph needle down on Benny Goodman's hit "Sing, Sing, Sing."

The drums pounded as Steve and Ruby stared at each other. They knew enough to wait until the high horns came in.

Then, at the first sound of a trumpet, they went into action, with Ruby effortlessly leading yet appearing to any casual observer to follow, deploying all her native powers of dissembling and fraudulence. The two of them rocked back and forth, pushing and pulling, keeping a steady amount of delicious tension between them. She's an all right dancer, Steve thought.

Ruby raised the ante by passively leading (but pretending to follow) Steve into more and more complicated tricks: jumping into his arms and having him slide her through his legs, having him twirl her around like a piece of spaghetti around a fork, having him fling her up in the air. They were doing beautifully, and things continued to get more and more interesting. Steve was actually having a great time. He'd never thought of himself as a dancer but now he would never think of himself as anything else. It's amazing, he thought, that I've never taken up a hobby I clearly have such natural talent for.

And it was just about that time that Ruby leapt bidirectionally, both three feet into the air and just about seven feet back, and flew clear into the exposed brick wall.

"Oh, dear," said Gildersleeve, observing the soft, pale, quivering lump of flesh that was Ruby. "Is she... is she all right?"

"I'm not sure" was the most honest assessment Steve could make.

#

That was it for Ruby. Steve was admitted into the ambulance by claiming he was her husband, but by the time they both got to the hospital, she was gone. Unconscious, she had no last words and Steve realized that he'd never before seen Ruby lack for a pithy turn of phrase. She just lost what little color she had and *stopped* right then and there on the ambulance floor, and the orderly riding in back held a mirror to her mouth and then pulled a sheet up over her head.

Steve was just floored. He knew he would miss his lunch partner every day—eating alone didn't suit him—but beyond that, there was a certain dance contest to be attended to. Not having paid his registration fee in advance since they were collecting it at the door, he supposed he could just drop out; but who knew what kind of musclebound, gun-toting monster would show up at his place if he did.

Steve was sitting at home staring at the floor and finishing up a fifth of rye, trying to figure out exactly what to do about the situation other than get drunk, when the phone rang. It was the gruff, disconsolate voice that had answered when Steve called about the ad. It now sounded even angrier, with an edge of impatience it hadn't had before.

"You tell the lady we don't do that," it said around both its cigar and its sandwich.

"Don't do what?" Steve asked warily, not wanting to reveal any more information than absolutely necessary.

"Don't do *that*," the voice repeated. "We're a clean house. We're a clean house, and we don't give extra cuts for any of that stuff."

"Extra cuts?" Steve said. "What did she... what did she offer to do, exactly?"

"Add a little extra excitement to the dance, is how she put it."

"What *kind* of excitement?"

"Excitement, you know. Do some fancy *French* dance numbers, catch my drift?"

"And naturally you said no."

"Of course I said no. What are you implying?" the voice demanded menacingly. "Look, I've been through a lot this year. This is the last thing I need. If the cops get wind of something like this actually happening, they'll close me down. Vice law. And I don't like it when cops get involved in things. It makes me mad. I do things people might not like. Temperamental things. Unpredictable things."

"OK, I get it."

"*Permanent* things," the voice hammered.

"I *get* it!"

"Now look, you seem like an upstanding type of guy, a real Andy Hardy. But your girlfriend or wife or whatever she is, she ain't no Rebecca of Sunnybrook Farm. I've known a lot of dames like that, and they're pretty good at making their husbands take the fall, so I'm telling you right now I ain't holding nothing against you personally but she. Has got. To go." Steve could hear him banging his fist against his palm for emphasis.

Steve paused for drama. He felt he had a right to. He'd been to hell and back. Ruby had had no next of kin—he'd always suspected as much, but it hadn't been confirmed until she passed—so Steve, being as close to her as anyone and a lawyer to boot, had spent much of the past two weeks signing releases, contracts, trust statements, disclosure and nondisclosure forms, and other papers. There was also a certain small matter of first degree manslaughter, a pending charge which his own lawyer assured him that he could beat due to Ruby's willfully dancing out of her own ability range. But right now, Steve was exhausted. He felt like if he were to sleep for the next seven days in a row it wouldn't be enough.

"She's gone," he said.

"What do you mean, she's gone? She skipped town?"

"No, she passed away," Steve explained.

"I see," said the voice, pausing to chew this over. "I'm sorry," he added, with what seemed genuine sincerity. Then the punch line: "Can you prove it?"

"Not beyond the shadow of a doubt, no."

"McGillicuddy ain't much for being lied to. If you say she's dead she better be a frigging doornail. Otherwise instead of one body there'll be two."

"Who's McGillicuddy!" Steve demanded. "You? Your boss? Or someone else I'll never get to meet in a million years, because he's too busy and too important?"

"You ask too many questions, mister," said the voice. "We'll take it on faith that your gal is dead. For now. If she turns up alive, we'll need a pretty good explanation."

"What about the Lovers Contest? Are we square? I never did pay an entry fee," Steve said.

"No, we're not square! You formally applied."

"But I didn't pay."

"It doesn't matter. You formally applied and now you need to attend."

"But I don't have another dance partner."

The voice shrugged - audibly, somehow. "That's your problem," he tossed off, and for good measure added "or else."

#

Never a particularly modest woman and always a practical one, Ruby had apparently put a lot of energy into her own funeral. A giant photograph of her face at its most radiant hovered over the crowd, most of whom Steve had never seen before, although he was surprised and in fact a little shocked to see Gildersleeve there, wearing yet another of his trademark sharkskin suits and even more oil in his hair. The rest of the attendees were a motley crew to say the least: the men tended to dress in outrageous colors with impeccably coiffed hair, while the women wore variations on black: classic, expensive, beatnik. But one got the sense that, rather than having dressed in black especially for the occasion, they simply clothed themselves that way all the time, whether out of minimalist simplicity or tidiness amid New York's grime.

Steve tried to stay as invisible as possible amid the loud laughter, gossip, flamboyant lighting of cigarettes, and other goings-on not usually characteristic of funerals, but Gildersleeve managed to corner him. "What's the meaning of this?" he remarked officiously. "I thought you would be in jail for manslaughter, not attending the victim's funeral."

"I'm out on bail," Steve assured him, "and my lawyer thinks I'll be cleared." Gildersleeve glowered at this. "I thought I should pay my respects," he added, "since I ate lunch with the 'victim' every Tuesday and Thursday for 10 years."

Gildersleeve sniffed. "Well, I'm glad *you* were able to attend," he said dubiously.

"By the way, how do *you* know Ruby outside of giving her dance lessons?" Steve asked, just making conversation.

Steve didn't anticipate what happened next. Gildersleeve melted like a candle. Tears started flowing from his eyes in a way Steve had rarely seen in a man and frankly never wished to see again. They stained Gildersleeve's beautiful, expensive suit and soaked his mustache.

"Ruby was the loveliest woman I have ever known," he said. He began weeping and bawling convulsively, and after a while Steve embraced him in spite of himself.

"How did you know each other?" Steve asked. He had assumed that the dance studio marked the first time they'd met.

"She was my *friend*, and friends are hard to find," said Gildersleeve.

"But how" Steve was about to ask, and then Gildersleeve was gone.

As Steve continued to looking around the room and observe the goings-on—there didn't seem to be any sort of itinerary, just general mingling and conversation under the watchful eyes of Ruby's huge photo—it occurred to him that she really had lived a rich, full life, even if it wasn't necessarily the life he would have picked for himself. He owed it to her, he thought, to do well in the contest, particularly the dance-off. Of course, he mused, no one in the history of lovers' contests had ever won by himself. But that wouldn't stop Steve from trying.

Soft, mournful music began to play from over in the corner, and Steve surmised that it was time for him to go. He made his way carefully through the rambunctious, carousing crowd, members of which continued to blow smoke in his face and laugh uproariously.

#

When the day came, Steve showed up at the address that the gruff, criminal-sounding, cigar-chomping voice on the phone had given to him. What he saw didn't surprise him. This highly-publicized, elaborate contest with a huge grand prize was being held in the basement of a third-rate office building with peeling paint and pigeons on the eaves. A straggling line of misfits, alcoholics, and people who probably shouldn't have gotten out of bed in the morning were queued up to get in, and an enormous doorman, more door than man and seven feet if he was an inch, looked each potential patron over and then admitted him. So far, no one had been rejected outright, although from the man's face and demeanor it certainly wasn't out of the question.

"Steve Weintraub," said Steve when it came his turn.

"You," the doorman sneered. "I should have known *you* would show up."

"Well, I did," Steve replied pointlessly. "Your boss said if I didn't there would be trouble."

"I don't *have* a boss," the doorman sneered even more nastily, and this time Steve instantly pegged his voice as the one behind the ad. The doorman took an enormous cigar out of his pocket and lit it with a kitchen match that he struck on the seat of his pants, staring down at Steve as though daring him to make an issue out of it.

Steve took this as permission, since the doorman was now paying more attention to the cigar than to him.

"Not so fast! This is a Lovers Contest," the doorman said. "I don't see anyone else with you."

"I'm entering the contest as a tribute to my good friend Ruby, who couldn't make it here tonight due to the fact that SHE KILLED HERSELF," Steve said, putting the most grinding, abrasive emphasis possible on the last part. He hadn't really thought about that until now. It had just come out of his mouth. After all, with Ruby's insane bravado and barely competent dancing, it really had been suicide, Steve told himself.

Inside, it was dank, smoky, and poorly ventilated. The "refreshments" advertised in the paper consisted of stale third-rate potato chips and a bowl of watery pink punch with a ladle in it. Even after his third glass of punch, Steve was hard-pressed to tell if it contained any booze.

There was a kissing contest, where Steve kissed a picture of Ruby (he lost); a declaration of undying love contest that involved tossing down a shot of horrible rotgut moonshine and then dedicating a toast, poem, or song to the beloved (Steve came in third place with an honorable mention); and then the dance contest. People booed Steve when he went onstage by himself, as though the only reason he was doing it was to claim the entire prize without needing to split it. One man even spit on him. But he was ready.

Steve stood stock still at the starting point. He was last since neither the doorman, who also appeared to be the party host master of ceremonies, nor the patrons seemed to really acknowledge his validity.

The needle dropped on the record player. The tune was a fast latin dance number with a rhythm Steve didn't even recognize. Some might have said it was a double-time samba, while others would have called it a more stylized, Europeanized version of the conga or a relaxed, late-night rhumba. There were even elements of tango in it, while something in the bass and the backbeat hinted at the new rock 'n' roll music all the high school girls had been screaming about lately.

"I'm going to give them the biggest show they've ever had in their life," Steve said, looking out at the social rejects and people who had been swept in off the street, their faces a sickly green under the horrible glare of the unfiltered hanging light bulb. "I'm going to do it myself. And I'm going to do it for Ruby."

To the bizarre music, which now included a bouzouki and an accordion as well as the traditional Latin instrumentation, all topped off with a vocalist singing a language he wasn't able to name or understand, Steve now began to dance his heart out. He jumped, he wobbled, he swung, and he pranced. He leapt and he soared, he bounced off the walls and the ceiling. He somehow managed to lead and follow at the same time. Not only did he do the waltz, the foxtrot, the gavotte and the minuet, the rhumba, the samba, the conga and the tango, the western swing and the Lindy and even the Charleston, he did about 17 dances that hadn't even been invented yet.

The audience, whose members were barely used to even a polite swing around the room at a wedding reception, stared at all this showmanship in thrilled, open-mouthed disbelief. Steve had clearly put a tremendous amount of time and effort into this, time and effort they themselves wouldn't dream of putting into such an arcane and impractical pursuit, and now it was paying off.

When Steve was done, he collapsed into one of the many scratched-up metal folding chairs that had been place haphazardly around the room. Sweat poured down his forehead at what seemed like a gallon a minute, and he hyperventilated as he wiped it off his face and into his hair, which became oily and matted with one big lock drooping down like he'd seen in newsreels of Hitler. He tried to brush it upwards but it fell right back down again. Puffing and panting, he looked around at the grudging smiles on the audience's faces, the women's coated with cheap makeup, the men's necks cradled by cheap ties.

The doorman/MC looked him over with a distasteful moue, but said the words that, had he not said them, would have made him a liar since Steve had so clearly and completely got the crowd on his side:

"The Winner and new World's Greatest Lover. Congratulations." He took Steve's hand and held it high over both their heads, while making a face as though someone was holding world's stinkiest blue cheese to his nose. The audience began clapping, at first slowly, the applause limited to one or two members; then it spread to everyone and became loud enough to fill the room. They had enjoyed Steve's little show, but more critically, it was something they knew damn well they could never do in a million years.

When Steve finally walked out of that building that night, his heart felt light and his wallet felt $2,500 heavier. The only thing missing was his friend. He didn't look forward to a lifetime of never seeing her again, and there was an anticlimactic feeling to having won a contest she was supposed to have participated in.

"I did it for you," he said to the sky, to the air, to the ground, to everywhere at once and no one in particular.

Now there was the matter of spending the prize money. Ruby had been a big fan of the Society for the Prevention of Cruelty to Animals, so that was an obvious choice. A foe of bigotry who was forever grieving about violence toward minorities, she also would have appreciated a donation to the NAACP, he felt, so he gave some of it away to them. Finally, he decided to keep some of the money for himself, as a reward for all the time and energy he'd put in. It was only fair, he thought, and besides he was tired of struggling. He took what he had doled out to himself as his share of the prize money, bought a tiny cottage in upstate New York, and set up a small business selling imprinted advertising specialties to other businesses.

Steve was also cleared of any charges against Ruby. The judge ruled that her death was partially due to her own carelessness, and partially due to negligence on the part of the dance studio.

One time, Steve went to visit Ruby's grave in a Brooklyn cemetery. She was buried in a Jewish cemetery even though she'd really only been half Jewish, on her mother's side. He poured some bourbon on the ground and read the tombstone:

RUBY MACBRIDE
1925-1955
SHE CAME. SHE SAW. SHE LEFT.

9 BOX OF TIME

The Great War had orphaned both Cecil and Prudence. This, more than any other reason, is why they were stuck with each other.

Cecil had been classified 4F during the war, but he knew exactly why the army didn't want to take him: he was black. He should have been grateful, he supposed, in a world where the army recruited Negroes as cannon fodder to fight the Germans and Japanese and Italians, all of whom had much bigger, better, more sophisticated weaponry against which paltry privates with cheap bayonets and misfiring rifles didn't stand a chance. But he had wanted, at least, the pride of serving his country, of dying in a heroic fashion and leaving the legacy of a clean tombstone.

Now, even that had been denied him. He was just a butler.

Then there was Prudence. An heiress and a woman of leisure, she had spent many years lunching at posh 5th Avenue restaurants with her cronies, never having worked a day in her life since she'd married her way up from the typing pool in an old-money legal firm. Her overworked husband had kicked the bucket while still in his early fifties, leaving her enough money to supply a dozen rich widows with mink stoles and chinchilla coats and lunches at Sardi's and dinners at 21.

But a widow has no real place during a war. She has no man to miss, no soldier on the front lines to think of during fundraisers and food drives, bond sales and victory garden plantings. Nor could she wangle a job at a factory or behind a cab wheel while the boys were overseas—much too old and inexperienced for that—and based on her physical condition, becoming a WAC or WAV herself was out of the question. So the war had left her behind, as well.

So Prudence and Cecil were both war orphans. They were just different sorts of war orphans from the kind that made the front cover of *Life* or the top story in the *March of Time* newsreel. But they did have each other.

Cecil had been Prudence's butler for the better part of 20 years, almost since the day her husband had died. Before that time Charles had had his own butler, Stevenson; but she hadn't liked him much and had given him his walking papers. Prudence had found Cecil while waiting in line for a movie and struck up a conversation. It turned out that they both enjoyed Bob Hope pictures, and things had blossomed from there. It certainly was not a romance that the two of them had—they'd never as much as held hands—but there was a certain kind of unspoken understanding that, if you'd asked either to define, they couldn't have done it.

Now Cecil and Prudence lingered over a lovely breakfast he had prepared, as he did each day: eggs over easy stripped with bacon, a sweet roll, and a small glass of fresh-squeezed grapefruit juice. Prudence, who hadn't much meat on her frame at all, just nibbled at the food, as usual, and barely put a mouse's teeth marks in the sweet roll; but it comforted her just to have it all in front of her every morning. Cecil, who put in a grueling, physical 10 hours every day of his life cooking and cleaning and generally attending to Prudence, tucked into his with great gusto and finished almost all of it, mopping up his egg yolk with giant pieces of sweet roll before they disappeared, neatly but completely, down his gullet.

"I found something yesterday I thought you might be interested in, Miz Prudence," Cecil said.

"How lovely," Prudence replied in her usual demure fashion. She wasn't just being polite, either. Over the years Cecil had found her an antebellum silver serving tray, pre-20th century Chinese and Japanese flower vases, and all manner of antiques, figurines, knick-knacks, and doodads for her display cases. He had a sharp, unerring eye for picking valuables out of trash piles, and he knew all the city's good antique stores as well as many in New Jersey and Connecticut.

"May I see it?" Prudence added, playing her part of their game with grace and aplomb.

"Certainly." And Cecil reached into a plain brown paper

shopping bag, which he had securely ensconced under the table before breakfast, and whipped out a small silver box.

"How wonderful," Prudence clapped. "Wherever did you find it?"

"From a vendor I hadn't had the opportunity to patronize before," Cecil intoned. "He had set up shop yesterday, in a former papaya juice stand."

"Fascinating."

"Even more fascinating is that I passed by the same store again this morning while walking Fifi, and it was once again a papaya juice stand, with no trace of the interim operator."

"Heavens to Betsy! Is this on the up and up?" Prudence looked at Cecil slyly through narrowed eyelids. "We're not talking about stolen merchandise, are we, my friend?"

"Certainly not, Miz Prudence," Cecil huffed. His reputation was spotless and he was intent on keeping it that way. "A perfectly legitimate purchase. A perfectly legitimate sale."

"That is what I like to hear," Prudence said. "So what is it, if I may ask? A music box? A snuff box? A cigarette case? A box for a child's toy puzzle? Or perhaps a purely ornamental affair with no purpose at all beyond being aesthetically pleasing, which it certainly is?" She smiled the pleased, and eager-to-please, smile of a child being presented with a rare and expensive sweetmeat.

"None of the above," Cecil replied with an air of exotic mystery. His voice had suddenly taken on a Caribbean or West Indian overtone, which Prudence knew to be perfectly fake, but she was thrilled nonetheless. "It's a Time Box."

"Oh, how darling! You mean it's for holding timepieces. Wristwatches, pocket watches, hourglasses. That sort of thing."

"No, ma'am. My understanding is that it's for holding time."

"I beg your pardon?" A raw skepticism, seldom seen, peeked out from behind Prudence's charm. "Holding what?"

"Holding time, or so said the man who sold it to me," said Cecil. "Miss Prudence, time is constantly flowing through our fingers. Our childhoods with their atomic vitality, pow! Gone before we know it. Our adolescences with their flowering passions, poof! Vanished. Our young adulthoods with their dreams, aspirations, ambitions: zap, zap, zap, gone, gone, gone. And in a blink we're old, you and I, suddenly vulnerable to every disease every catalogued and a few no one's even thought of, mere steps from the end of the line, where there's no time at all because it's slipped through our grasp like greased mercury. Miz Prudence, didn't you ever want to hold onto time? To stop it, right in its tracks? To sock it away, like jewelry or love letters or anything else we don't want to lose?"

"Well yes... yes of course I have, Cecil...that's a sweet thought." She pierced her grapefruit half with a serrated teaspoon specifically designed for that purpose.

"It is, it *is*," Cecil nodded sagely. "But then again, it *isn't*."

"Come again?"

"And in the immortal words of Mr. Thomas Wright Waller, one never knows, do one?"

And Cecil passed the Time Box with great pomp and circumstance to Prudence, who accepted it hesitantly and with some alarm.

"Thank you, Cecil," she said, managing a tone halfway between puzzlement and gratitude, as though she were accepting from an obstetrician a baby with a beautiful face but no legs. "You are most kind and I'll, I'll...use it in good health."

"Please remember me when you do," he said. "And now, if you don't mind, ma'am, today is Thursday, my day off; and so I'll be on my way, for a day of gentlemanly relaxation, and will see you tomorrow morning for breakfast at seven a.m. sharp."

"Oh! I almost forgot," said Prudence. In fact, she forgot every week, and Cecil had to remind her. "Enjoy the day, then," she cried, and handed him a ten-dollar bill from her personal change purse for pocket money, as was her custom.

And then he was gone, much more quickly than usual. Almost as if he were *clearing* out, Prudence thought. As if something were going to happen that he didn't want to stay around *for*.

Once Cecil was gone, leaving behind him an eerie and lonely air of quiet, Prudence stared out into the distance. And there *was* a distance to stare into. Her apartment was enormous, particularly for New York City. The ceiling was two typical people high and three times as tall as Prudence herself, who was a step away from being a bona fide midget. What was she doing rattling around in such an enormous apartment, when an efficiency would have felt much cozier and would have been easier to get around in, too? She was so very alone. Just the sheer volume of space called attention to the fact. And yet, if not for all the space, where would she put all of her collections? Empty perfume bottles, samplers she'd crocheted when her fingers were still flexible enough, Hummel figures of kewpie-eyed boys and girls, photographs of long-gone relatives in equally antique frames, hundred-year-old oak showcase shelves filled with indescribables. Without all of these little friends, she would surely feel even more alone, and where would she put them?

She fondled the silver box Cecil had given her before he'd hightailed it out the door. A box of time? What a load of nonsense. Cecil was usually so sensible, and in fact Prudence relied on his sensible nature since from girlhood on she'd been a flighty fool, so much so that it had taken her 70 years even to realize it. But "box of time" not only wasn't sensible, it was barely English.

Still, she thought, she was an enlightened individual who didn't believe in magic, or voodoo, or even religion very much although she went to Episcopalian services on Sundays for social reasons. So what was there to be afraid of?

Prudence opened the box.

#

In 1885, a five-year-old girl lay sunning herself under a magnolia tree. She was wearing her fancy white Sunday cotton dress, which her mother had had the servants tailor especially for her. It had only taken three of them to measure her for it, design it, sew it, and alter it to fit exactly. ("Exactly" being relative, for she was still growing.)

With her eyes closed, Prudence lay back and listened to the cicadas. Their click-chirp clatter sounded like conversation, and she translated it in her mind. "Hello, how are you?" "I am fine, thank you. Nice to meet you." "Would you like to stay for tea?" As far as she knew, the cicadas were all having a splendid party and she was glad to attend as a guest.

Then Prudence heard a noise that was not cicadas. It was louder, and deeper, and shook the ground with a kind of muscular panic. It was horses, and their hard, rapid gallop was quickly encroaching. Prudence was used to horses, but not like this. This was the sound of horses in terror, being whipped within an inch of their lives.

Prudence opened her eyes and snapped her head up. What she saw made her heart beat a mile a minute, not least because she had no idea exactly what was going on or why. There were three men riding three white horses, all of them wearing pointy hoods with eyeholes cut out and sheets draped about their bodies. Their horses were wearing the confederate flag, which Prudence knew from her father and school teacher had been outlawed, though that hadn't stopped many people from displaying one.

Tied to the last horse was the body of a large, well-muscled black man. The man was clearly dead and his corpse was bloody. The horse was dragging him along over the ground, bumping him on the rough, rocky soil, adding insult to his fatal injury.

The horses stopped in front of Prudence. Her heart beat even faster. She figured, very logically, that she might be next, that these hooded ghost-monsters might kill her and tie a rope to her and drag her from their enormous white horses as well. She squinted her eyes tight and wrapped her arms around her head, curling into a fetal position. *I'm not here, I'm not here, I'm not here,* she thought, like an apprentice witch casting a magic spell. *I'm somewhere else, I'm somewhere else, I'm somewhere else.*

An amused, droll voice interrupted her incantation. "Is your daddy home, little girl? I've got something he might like to see." And he laughed a rich, hearty laugh. Prudence opened her eyes to the frontmost rider, who was lighting a cigar and smoking it through a mouth slit in his hood. "Can you run and get him for me?"

"My daddy ain't home," Prudence said truthfully. She really thought she was going to wet her pants right then and there.

"How about your momma, then?" The man's amused tone was almost affectionate, protective, as though Prudence were his own little girl or maybe his niece.

"My momma's home," Prudence answered.

"Well, I think I got something here your momma would like to see just as much or maybe even more," the man said. "We done her a right good deed. We done her a favor she ain't never gonna forget and I think she'd like to see it." He sounded very proud of himself. "Whyncha go get her now?"

"All right," Prudence said, and she got up and marched into the house to the rhythm of the cicadas' hum. She really did think she was going to throw up. "Momma," she said uncertainly. "There's a man who's here to see you."

"Coming," her mother called. She was all the way over on the other side of the house, which was quite large. She stepped crisply and firmly, clutching a tall glass of sweet tea. When she saw the men waiting outside, she turned pale as the sheets on the riders themselves and paler than their horses.

"Good day, ma'am," said the man with the cigar. "We thought you'd be downright pleased. We done you a favor and we wanted to give you peace of mind: undeniable proof." He gestured toward the slack, black body tethered to the rearmost horse.

"Oh my God," said Prudence's mother.

"He raped you, ma'am," said the cigar smoker, "and now we're just returning the favor. We know it can never bring back your dignity or your female—"

"You get out of here!" Prudence's mother screamed. Her face had gone from ghost-white to bright scarlet and she was screaming at the top of her lungs, about an octave higher than her usual voice, an insane animal roar one would expect to hear from a hyena or rabid coyote. "You get out of here right now! Oh my God! What have you done, what have you done? Oh my Jesus!"

"But ma'am—" the cigar smoker started in.

"Are you deaf? Get out of here! Get off my property right now, you— you—bastard!" It was not the worst word her mother could think of, Prudence knew, but it was the worst she was willing to say.

The lead horseman shook his head through the sheet and rode away. "Some people got no gratitude," he muttered through his sheet, as he motioned to his two comrades to follow him off the premises. He took an extra-long pull from his cigar and flicked it away, still glowing, before kicking his heels into his horse's white flanks.

"Was that man... dead?" Prudence said. She had heard stories of dead people coming alive from friends and particularly from her brothers, who seemed to be obsessed with skulls and ghosts and cemeteries.

"Yes," sniffed her mother, barely audible over the cicadas, which seemed to have grown in number and volume since the horsemen left.

Prudence's eyes widened. "Who was he?" she asked.

"He was a friend of mine," Prudence's mother said defiantly.

"Was he a friend of daddy's?" Prudence asked innocently.

"No, darling," said Prudence's mother. "No, he was not. But he was a friend of *mine*."

"Oh," said Prudence.

"He was a very good friend, and they did a horrible thing to him," her mother added. And then she stopped talking, mopped her eyes with a lace handkerchief, and, while Prudence was watching, simply collapsed physically, posture dissolving into thin air until she seemed to be about half her former height. Her facial structure also appeared to fall apart, muscles going slack and cheekbones appearing to drop until her now red, blotchy face was completely unrecognizable.

"Momma?" said Prudence.

"Yes, baby," her mother was barely able to mutter under her breath.

"I love you," said Prudence uncertainly, more as a question and a request for reassurance than a proclamation.

"I love you, too, baby," said her mother.

And she picked Prudence up, and drew her up to her bosom, and her tears fell onto Prudence's forehead, first one drop or two, then a steady, wet, salty flow that Prudence could feel and taste.

"I'm sorry, momma," said Prudence.

"You're so sweet, baby," her mother murmured between sobs. "Why? Why would you be sorry? You didn't do anything."

"I called you," she said. "I made you see it. You didn't have to see it, but I made you." And she started crying, too, even though she didn't quite understand why, but her mother was crying and so it seemed like the right thing to do. The whole world seemed incredibly sad to her, even though she didn't know this man and even though she knew she wasn't supposed to care about him because he wasn't white and was therefore to be thought of as more animal than human and had probably just been a slave only recently, since everyone knew slavery had only been outlawed around the time Prudence was born and there were still a lot of people who wanted it to be law again.

"Momma?" said Prudence, who had never been to a funeral in her short life. "What was his name?"

"His name was Caesar," her mother said.

"Will Caesar ever un-die?" said Prudence.

"No, baby," said her mother. "Once you die, that's it, honey. There's no such thing as un-dying. Caesar is in heaven with the angels now. And Jesus," she added perfunctorily.

Her mother looked skyward with dull, hopeless eyes. Prudence joined her and looked in the same direction. She looked hard, trying to see what her mother so clearly saw. She saw nothing but the ornately trimmed ceiling.

"I don't see Jesus," Prudence said, "and I don't see any angels either."

"Keep on looking, baby. Look harder and harder, and you will."

There was a brief pause as Prudence tried to see what her mother saw. Cicada music filled the vacuum.

"Is Caesar an angel now, too?" Prudence asked.

"Yes, baby," her mother said. "Yes, he definitely is."

And Prudence's mother took her liquid-filled, unfocused eyes off the ceiling to look out into the distance, in the direction where the horsemen had galloped off, and she held Prudence tight; and she stayed in that position for the rest of the day and well into the night, even after many of the servants, and her very formally dressed husband, had passed by and gently asked her if she was all right, was there anything they could do for her, could they get her a julep, could they get her a sweet tea, could they get her some sal ammonia, and so on and so forth like that.

There was nothing anyone could do for a woman whose one true love had died at the hands of hate.

#

Prudence lifted her boulder-heavy head off the hard metal of the box. She'd fallen asleep on top of it at seven in the morning and now, looking out the window, she noticed that night had fallen. Her face burned where the box's sharp edges and corners had dug into her fragile century-old skin, and she was afraid to look in a mirror lest she see a giant box-shaped blemish framing her face.

Prudence had not only never recalled anything from as early as five, she had never even remembered anything from before thirteen. Everything else had been a big, neutral, gray blank. But that, what she had just experienced—"dream" seemed the wrong word—had been very, very real. She could still smell the sweat stink of the horses and the evil cigar smoke. The rhythmic cicada hum still rang in the air. The taste of her mother's tears lingered.

But perhaps most palpable, oddly, was the sadness. The way her mother's face turned pale, then flushed, and went slack, devoid of tone and expression as though someone had stolen her soul. The shaking and the suddenly-poor posture and the aging of 50 years within the space of 10 minutes. That was what was most real to Prudence. That's what she, not even recalled, but simply *saw* right in front of her as she stared out the window into the Manhattan night.

A Box of Time, Prudence thought. A gift I didn't want to receive. A time I didn't want to have to relive. A memory best forgotten. An event that should have stayed well-buried beneath the detritus of the years.

She felt weak, and alone. She got up to make some tea.

Prudence could feel herself going through the motions as though operating a marionette from a great distance: filling the kettle, lighting the gas burner, carefully measuring tea into the teapot. She double-checked to make sure the gas burner was lit, that the flame had taken. She wasn't ready to go, not that way, not yet.

There was a knock at the front door. "Come in," she mumbled, knowing from the sound of the knock exactly who it was. The door was still unlocked, as it had been when Cecil had left that morning at seven; although he carried a key as part of his butler's duties, he didn't have to use it just then.

"Hello, Miz Prudence," he said jovially. "I know it's my day off, but I came to fix you dinner since you looked a little hungry this morning." It was his face-saving voice; he had come to do no such thing, but that was all right with Prudence. "How was the Box O' Time? Have you been enjoying it? Did it work like the man said or was it a humbug? If it was, you know, I can try to take it back. Only," he added, "I'm not exactly sure if a papaya juice stand does take returns."

"There's no need to take it back," Prudence said glumly. "It worked like a charm."

"Something tells me there's more here than meets the eye," said Cecil, "else why would you sound so melancholy and depressed? If you don't mind my asking," he added quickly, not wanting to appear more nosy than a butler had a right to.

"No," Prudence said lackadaisically. "I don't mind. Cecil, how long have you been working for me?"

"Nigh unto 20 years, Miz Prudence," Cecil said proudly.

"Why don't you take the rest of the night off?" Prudence said. "Why don't you take off until further notice, as a matter of fact?" She said all of this with great reluctance. She loved Cecil and wasn't sure what she'd do without him.

"Why, Miz Prudence," Cecil replied. "It's not like you to talk that way. You sure you feeling all right? I can try to return that Box O'Time and get a refund," he said again, reaching gingerly for the box as though it might bite him. Prudence put a hand on it and gently shooed him away from it.

"It's all right, Cecil," she said. "This was an excellent and very thoughtful gift. Please don't return it, or take it away. It's already given me so much."

"Yes, Miz Prudence."

"Now please, go home."

"But this is my home, Miz Prudence."

"Then you must find another. Where do you stay on your day off?"

"At the YMCA, ma'am, or sometimes with a friend."

Prudence reached for the pocketbook hanging over her chair. She fished around inside it for a while and came up with a huge handful of cash. "Please take this and find yourself a decent place to stay," she said. "I don't want you coming back here."

"But -"

"I won't take no for an answer, Cecil. You have to live your life. Not mine."

"Does this mean I'm fired from my job, ma'am?"

"You're an intelligent and healthy gentleman. You'll easily find jobs that pay many times what I've been paying. Now please, go."

Cecil nodded solemnly. "You'll be all right tending to yourself?" he asked, rather suspiciously. "Making your own meals and tending to your own personal needs and so forth?"

"That's my concern," Prudence said. "I'll miss you, Cecil. Goodbye." She put out a hand, and he took it and shook it for perhaps a moment longer than either normally considered correct.

"Goodbye to *you*, Miz Prudence," he said sadly, and tipped his hat. Then he was gone.

Prudence stared deep into the Box of Time. Had she been too hasty? No, she thought. If anything, she'd waited too long. Cecil was more capable than she, in every way: physically stronger, brighter, more resourceful, more imaginative, more patient and less whiny, more even-keeled. A better individual in every way. That he had found work as a butler was a combination of the bad hand he had been dealt and the way he had chosen to play it, nothing more.

Now, he had a chance to start fresh. In her head, Prudence added up the money she had given him. About a thousand dollars and change, she thought. That ought to last a while in, even in New York with inflated 1950's prices.

She thought back on her experience with the Box of Time. Already it was starting to seem like another life, fading from the direct experience it had been just moments before. But the crushing sadness she felt in her mother's arms, the bewilderment at seeing a black body dragged down a dirt road by a white horse, the shock of seeing a gruff-voiced man smoke a cigar through a ghost sheet - that feeling, she knew, would never fade.

Prudence's phone rang. She rose, every joint aching with electric pain, and answered it.

"Hello?"

"This is Mrs. O'Hara, the landlady. I'm not quite sure how to tell you this. Your butler, the... Negro man who comes and cooks for you every day? Your help? I think... I think I just saw him get hit by a bus."

"Excuse me?

"He's lying in the street and doesn't look well. He doesn't seem to be moving. I... I thought you should know."

"Thank you," Prudence said. She hung up the phone and looked out the window. A crowd was gathering already. An ambulance siren could be heard, and the bus driver was looking down helplessly on Cecil, his neat flat visored uniform cap over his standard-issue bow tie.

Prudence tottered over to the stove, using all the energy she could muster. It wasn't much. She turned on the gas for all the burners and the oven. This time, she did not light it.

She wandered back to the table, sat comfortably in the chair, and looked deep into the Box of Time.

"Take me back," she said. "Take me back. Oh, take me back."

10 BONUS STORY: DINNER AT TAGLIA'S (AFTER TRUMAN CAPOTE)

The first time I saw Emily, I was on my third beer and she was probably on her fourth martini. She could hold them well enough that I was never really sure. We met at The Blue Swan, a once-tony place that had seen better days back when Tommy Dorsey was big. Now Dorsey was an off-the-radar has-been and so was the Swan. A woman of a certain age, but definitely over my own, was trying to chat me up over the din of a ridiculous record, of which the only lyrics I could make out were "Man oh man" repeated endlessly.

"What's eating you, dear?'" she screamed into my ear. This time I could hear her, barely. I could also smell her Chanel No. 5, especially near the neck.

"I'm all right," I yelled over the record, eyeing said neck, which contained its share of craters and valleys, and moving my eyes quickly down to her au courant blue sequined cocktail dress. "And you?"

The truth was that I wasn't all right. Two hours ago, I'd lost my job. I had only been working as a mailroom clerk and my business aspirations hadn't really been any higher, set as I was on what I believed to be the loftier goal of Successful Writer. I had, however, appreciated the regular paychecks, the rough comraderie, and the smoke breaks with often raunchy-tongued secretaries. Now all that was over, and after only three weeks—a record-breaker for me in an unlucky streak that included employment periods of seven months, three months, and six weeks. My ability to hold a job was wearing thinner and thinner, helped along by a caustic mouth and my willingness to use it on anyone above or below me.

"I got fired today," I yelled, figuring since I wasn't particularly interested in making a good impression I may as well throw caution to the winds. "From my fourth job this year." I held up my half-empty beer mug in a toast. "Here's to new opportunities," I declaimed merrily, pouring the rest of the beer down my throat.

"Indeed," she agreed and swooped her martini toward mine, but without our actually touching glasses. She, too, finished her drink in a single swallow. I didn't especially like where this was going, seeing as how she was old enough to be my aunt if not my mother; but, as I may have mentioned, I had nothing else going on that night.

"Emily," she said, and I told her my name as well though I'm not sure she caught it over the blare of the jukebox, into which the fleshy, gum-popping barmaid continued to pump company quarters.

"Maybe we ought to go someplace with a little less collateral damage," I added, nodding toward the door just in case my meaning wasn't clear. I put down my empty mug, and she followed me out the door into the night.

As soon as the door was behind us, Emily whipped a cigarette out of a long, gold case. I intentionally say "gold" and not "golden" or "gold-plated." My grandfather having been in the business, I can spot costume jewelry a mile away. The case was also encrusted with something glittery and white. "I want you to know," Emily said, "I may be married but I'm not desperate. You'll get no more than the standard amount."

"The standard amount of what?" I asked, now beginning to suspect it was all bull.

"Do we have to play coy about everything? You're a big boy. Money, darling," she elaborated. "For fucking me."

I hadn't been that long out of Illinois—Springfield, not even Chicago—and the idea of paying for sex struck me as amoral, even insulting, particularly if I wasn't the one doing the paying. I was probably even about to blurt out "What kind of a boy do you think I am" or some such nonsense, but then I thought about the price of New York rents, and my repeated firings from jobs a sleepwalker could have kept, and what had been an affront started to sound like a pretty good opportunity.

"I'm a writer, not a company man," I pondered. "My business reputation is in the sewer. Why not flush a couple more times and send it on its way?"

I thought all of this in the blink of an eye, and then I turned back to Emily, looking her straight in the eyes through a fresh cloud of her cigarette smoke, and asked "Where do I sign?"

"Written contracts don't really enter into it," she replied, "though your naiveté is charming. Charm goes a long way with me. So does literacy, by the way. The last one couldn't hold up his end of a conversation."

"The last one?" I did raise an eyebrow at that, couldn't help it. "How many have there been, exactly?"

"Darling, what does it matter, really? Think of me as a man if it'll set your mind at ease."

"Not if we're going to be spending much time in bed, it won't."

"Which reminds me, my place or yours?" she said. "My place will work just fine even though my husband is there, seeing as how he spends nearly all his time passed out on the couch with a bottle of Four Roses."

I was beginning to get the picture. "What does your husband do for a living? I asked, mostly to make idle conversation.

"He drinks, darling, just as I said."

"They pay him for that, do they?"

"As much for that as for anything. Not that I object. He gets to enjoy his favorite hobby, and I get to enjoy mine."

"Well, call me an incurable romantic," I said, "but I'd like to get to know you just a little before we embark on this arrangement. What would you say to a late dinner? On me, just in case you think I'm trying to cadge some free food or something."

"I've already eaten, dearest, but if it'll make you happy, I'm glad to have a salad and another martini."

"It's a deal," I said. I turned the corner and headed to a small noodle-and-red-ink place in Little Italy that I used to frequent when I was dating Sophia Masciarelli. They had salad, they had alcohol. I figured that would do the trick.

"It's a ten-block walk," I told Emily, "if you can restrain yourself for that long."

"Don't be vulgar, darling," she replied crisply, head held high, cheeks more than a tad flushed. She made a point of straightening her cocktail dress, repositioning her wrap so she wouldn't freeze half to death in the wind.

#

It being one in the morning, Taglia's was something of a ghost town. We were the only customers there, the crew now consisting of one waiter, who was also the manager, maitre'd, and quite possibly owner, and a cook who doubled as a dishwasher. I'd never been in that late, but figured I'd take my chances with the food. My idea was that a posh society matron such as Emily had probably never been in a dive like this one and so would be bowled over by the exotic peasant nature of the food. I was wrong on both counts, but it wasn't the food she'd been bowled over by.

"Well, hel-lo, Fillipi," Emily fairly sang when the waiter/owner came by to take our order. "How's tricks?"

"Tricks they good, Miss Emily," Fillipi replied in an exaggerated phony accent that would put Chico Marx to shame. "How-a you been? How long now, eight months?"

"Nine, but who's counting," she smoldered. I was beginning to feel more than a little jealous, without putting my finger on why. Yes, this was a purely business arrangement and an as-yet-unconsummated one at that, but I'd be damned if some spaghetti slinger were going to muscle in on my territory.

"How do you two even know each other?" I said, making no effort to hide my annoyance. "I've been coming here for years."

"So've I," Emily replied, "but it doesn't seem to make much difference to Fillipi here." She fondled his chin. "We're just very good friends. Now."

"We had a few good laughs together, Miss Emily."

"We certainly did," she said, and I'll spit on my mother's grave if there wasn't a damned tear in her eye when she said it.

"I'll have spaghetti a la marinara," I said with an edge in my voice I knew probably wasn't becoming, "with extra parmesan and a glass of chianti. The lady will have a salad and a martini." Filippi dutifully took the order, winked brazenly at Emily, and strolled back to the kitchen.

"Maybe we shouldn't have come here," I said in a wounded tone.

"Don't be silly, darling," Emily said. "I can't believe you're actually jealous. He is a spaghetti waiter, after all. I'm here with you, not him; and this isn't the most uncomplicated situation to begin with." She flashed her ring at me. "Perhaps if you're the jealous type we should say goodbye here and now."

"The funny thing is, I'm usually not." Filippi brought the glass of

Chianti and I sipped at it, but it was tannic, bitter.

"You'll learn to be a bit more sophisticated," Emily said, lighting up over her martini. "At least, I hope so. You have so much to give in...other areas." She reached out and felt my bicep through my coat. I'd been spending time at the gymnasium. "My, my, my," she said. "I think I'll be patient enough to give you a lesson or two."

"I'm not just off the plane from the prairie," I protested.

"You do understand this will be a business relationship, not an affair of the heart? We both have needs. As long as they're mutually fulfilled, everyone stays happy."

"Sure, only am I the only one...fulfilling your needs?"

"That really doesn't enter into the picture, darling, and again must tell you that if it matters to you, you may not be cut out for the job, which would be quel domage." Filippi brought the food and she attacked her salad hungrily, as though she hadn't eaten in days. I thought maybe I should have ordered her a plate of lasagna in spite of her comment.

"I'm cut out for it fine," I said. "But at least for a while, if you're seeing anyone else, I don't want to know about it."

"As long as it's a two-way street, darling."

"Fair's only fair," I shrugged.

And that was it for a bit. I toyed with my spaghetti, twirling it around my fork the way I'd seen dogs do in Lady and the Tramp, and Emily dug into her salad like it was the last food on Earth. We didn't talk because there wasn't much to talk about, and I assumed we didn't really share any common interests anyway. That turned out to be the case, though when I told her I was a writer with a book of stories under my belt there was no end of cheerleading.

Eventually we finished our dinner, whereupon Filippi came and took our plates himself. I guess he was also playing the role of busboy on top of maitre'd, waiter, and swarthy Mediterranean lover. Then, as quickly as he'd left, he came right back with two enormous parfait glasses filled with spumoni. And when I say filled, I mean filled: the amount of ice cream towering over the glasses was at least equal to the amount inside the glasses themselves. Giant chunks of dark chocolate, dried fruit, and cake were visible in what was clearly a house-made spumoni and not some store-bought knockoff.

"Well, well, well," Emily said. "Filippi, you cad! If I didn't know better I'd think you were trying to win me back."

"You caught me! With a beautiful and charming lady such as yourself, how can I not at least give it, how you say in English, the old college try?"

"Honestly, Filippi, you simply tear me to pieces." All of this was getting just a little too cute for words, and Filippi's obsequious charm, which I initially found only slightly off-putting, had now turned completely obnoxious.

"Listen, friend," I said, standing up. A corn-fed midwesterner, I was about a head taller than Filippi and now took full advantage of my stature. "My patience is just about at an end. I don't know if you happen to have noticed it, but Emily and I are on a date. I understand that you've have remained friends. I think we'd all like to keep it that way. Now, the food is fine here and I appreciate your excellent service, but you'd be doing us all a favor if you'd keep the amorous chitchat to a minimum."

Filippi turned about seven shades paler. A crestfallen look of shame took over his face. He looked as though he was about ready to go confess to the pope himself. "I'm very sorry, mister," he said to me, and then turned and apologized to Emily as well. Emily smiled, winked, and lightly waved him off.

"Darling, you got yourself all worked up," Emily said, wagging a finger at me. I thought this was more than a little presumptuous not to mention motherly, but I just kept thinking of the weekly paycheck and it didn't seem too bad.

"Sorry if I was out of line," I said. "There's just something about him that rubs me the wrong way. I can't put my finger on it. I don't mean to hurt your feelings... I know the two of you were, ah, together."

"Yes," Emily said, "though that's all water under the Triborough Bridge."

"Mind if I ask why the two of you broke up, exactly?"

"I don't quite recall, darling. Something perhaps about him being a tad, what's the word I'm hunting for, pushy. He's not the shy retiring sort as you can see, and subtlety isn't really his specialty. He had trouble taking a hint and still does, but he's harmless enough. I just laugh and treat it all as a funny little game."

"Hilarious," I said.

We finished as much of our brobdingnagian dishes of spumoni as we could shovel into our mouths, and on Emily's cue we even shoveled some of it into each other's mouths. Someone might as well have posted a large neon sign over us with an arrow saying ROMANTIC COUPLE HERE. Then, of course, there were the equally enormous cups of cappuccino, intensely strong Italian coffee with giant mounds of creamy milk foam that gave us both ghostly white mustaches.

And then the meal was over. I tried to get the check, but Emily was too quick for me, handing a wad of cash thicker than her arm over to Filippi before I could say pasta fazool. I tried to parry her wallet with my own but she would have none of it. Well, why pretend, I thought as I put my money away. I swept my feelings of shame under the rug of my ambitions, where I hoped they would stay for at least the remainder of the evening.

Something seemed wrong to me, though. The bill had been big, but nowhere near as big as the stack of cash Emily had left. Even allowing for a generous tip, there was still an enormous difference that couldn't be accounted for.

"What was that all about?" I said. "You're not still supporting him, are you?"

"Darling, I never did," she replied. "He wouldn't have been worth the trouble. He's got as many women as there are days of the week." I believed her, too.

"But then what—"

"Shh," she said, a little patronizingly. "Some things were meant to remain mysteries."

Well, I didn't think so. As a writer, which I may have mentioned is my profession even though I'm on an involuntary extended hiatus, I believe mysteries are just fine for readers but not for me. So I made it a point to stay observant, tense and on edge right up until we left. I didn't see anything untoward, however. Filippi took Emily's money and that was that.

It just happened to be a lot of money.

We sat there for what seemed like an eternity. I looked past Emily, trying to maintain an air of attractive aloofness and boredom, while she looked right at me, taking in what women have told me are my boyishly charming looks.

"And so to bed," I ventured, figuring the shortest distance between two points is generally a line.

"You're a bit of an eager beaver, aren't you?"

"That's my line," I smirked.

"You're a bit of a gutter mouth too," Emily remarked. "If you're going to spend much time with me you'll learn to be a gentleman. Well, everyone starts somewhere, I suppose."

"I suppose."

"We'll have to get you a better sport coat, too," she sniffed, pinching my elbow-patched corduroy jacket as though skin contact might give her a disease. "Maybe a couple."

"Whatever you say." The lights began to snap off one by one as Filippi shut the place down from his central command in the kitchen. "Time to go?"

"I'd say so," Emily opined lazily. She stubbed out her cigarette and stood up, waiting for me to drape her wrap around her shoulders, which I did. As we stood up to leave, I noticed Filippi nonchalantly but very quickly moving out of the kitchen to take a spot by the front door.

"So nice to see you, Miss Emily," he said. "And very nice to meet you as well, sir. I hope you enjoyed your meal. Have a lovely evening."

"We plan to," I said pointedly. I stepped away, but kept an ear out.

Then a funny thing happened. Filippi lowered his voice to a stage whisper. I couldn't hear everything he was saying, but it sounded like "How'd I do?" and "I hope it worked," even mentioning Lee Strasberg and The Actors' Studio. More striking than the content of what was said were the tone and accent. There was no trace of Sicily this time, just the plummy, practiced, pan-Atlantic tones of the Broadway actor—Standard American dialect, equal parts London and New York. And there was a definite fey quality about the voice, as well. I'm not saying I'm positive Fillipi was homosexual, but neither was I entirely sure at that point that his name was Filippi.

I'm no genius, but this was all pointing to something. The pieces arranged and rearranged themselves in my brain like Scrabble tiles, looking for a possible word to form, something that actually appeared in the dictionary.

Then it hit me.

"You hired him to do that," I said angrily. I stopped us in our tracks. So what if I caused a ruckus on a street corner? I'd done worse. Three or four passersby began to stare.

"Darling, you're making a scene," Emily said.

"Blame yourself," I replied. "You find a waiter who needs an extra buck and pay him to play the part of your spurned lover just so you can feel desired? So I'll become jealous and fawn all over you? That's it, isn't it? You wanted to appear to be a valued commodity so you created a stalking horse. And not just any stalking horse but the pride of the stable! A graduate of the Actor's Studio yet. Next you'll tell me you had Elia Kazan film the whole thing for posterity."

If she was mortified, she wasn't showing it. I'd never seen such self-control in my life, her performance equal to or exceeding Filippi's. Unless, of course, life had managed to stub out any trace of emotion in her, just like one of her used-up Nat Sherman cigarettes, leaving only an elegant, sexually needy shell.

"Do you want to earn your pay or not?" she said coolly.

"Yes." I cast my eyes downward at the gum- and trash-filled street, like a boy who'd been caught filching from the cookie jar.

I studied a Greek-motif coffee cup from the Automat. "We are happy to serve you," it said.

That was me. Happy to serve.

And so our arrangement began in earnest. We were equals now, participating in an even exchange: my services for her crisp, green, postwar American dollars. She couldn't put one over on me even when enlisting the help of her semi-out-of-work actor friends, and she knew it. Meanwhile, I pulled my weight every step of the way, but business it was and business it would stay.

We hailed a cab and took it to her apartment uptown. I have to say it was quite a way from the YMCA and the cold-water walk-ups I'd split with beatniks and college kids. both in terms of distance and, well, everything else.

I looked out the cab window at the city skyline. I could see the Empire State building, the Flatiron, the stars, and some clouds backlit by an enormous fat yellow full moon. It was all too dramatic, like a picture drawn by a little kid. I couldn't shrug off the feeling that I was being set up for something.

I was going home with a woman who was paying me to sleep with her, probably against her own better judgment, although you wouldn't know it from the way she was snuggling her head against the hollow between my neck and shoulder in the back seat of the cab. I tried to remember which aftershave I'd used. I have to admit I felt nothing but a happy surge of opportunity—the same feeling I got when I sold cars and knew I had a sucker on the line, or when I was about to get legitimately lucky with one of the intellectual artist's models who hung around the seedier joints in the Village.

"Wait until you see my place," Emily said. "I'm an interior designer, you know. You'll be able to tell as soon as you set foot inside. And I'm going to make a special room just for you. A masculine room full of oh so masculine things. I think I might even have a line on where to get a pair of antlers for the wall."

"Don't forget to include a kibble bowl on the floor and a sandbox for when nature calls," I said sourly, figuring I had nothing to lose at this point.

"Oh, now don't let's be bitter," she said, not moving her head from its niche. "Think of this as a romance with pay. Really, what could be better? And there will certainly be paid time off. I insist on it, in fact."

That was a better deal than I'd had on most regular jobs—and I'd held a few including driving a cab myself, mover, baker, soda jerk, gas pumper, coffee slinger, selling everything from ad space to zither strings—so I decided to shut up. I sniffed the air. It smelled like Chanel #5 and stale tobacco, with an undernote of gin. It was Eau de Emily and I was all right with it. Why wouldn't I be? In the most expensive, dangerous city in the world, she'd saved my life.

Or ended it. I wasn't yet sure which.

ABOUT THE AUTHOR

Dave Dumanis is the author of *Alphabetical Disorder, The Soft Pink and White Bunnyrabbit Story, Cream, Mona Liebowitz: an Artless Novel, Obsessed,* and *A Plague of Boils.* He lives in San Francisco with his wife and daughter.

CPSIA information can be obtained at www.ICGtesting.com
Printed in the USA
LVOW10s1016010813

345785LV00010B/68/P